PENGUIN CLA

SIR GAWAIN AND THE GREEN KNIGHT

BERNARD O'DONOGHUE was born in Cullen, County Cork in 1945. Since 1965 he has lived in Oxford, where he teaches medieval English at Wadham College. He has published five volumes of poetry, as well as books on the language of modern poetry and on medieval literature. His anthology of medieval European love poetry, *The Courtly Love Tradition*, was published in 1982.

Sir Gawain and the Green Knight

Translated and introduced by
BERNARD O'DONOGHUE

PENGUIN BOOKS

PENGUIN CLASSICS

Published by the Penguin Group
Penguin Books Ltd, 80 Strand, London WC2R 0RL, England
Penguin Group (USA) Inc., 375 Hudson Street, New York, New York 10014, USA
Penguin Group (Canada), 90 Eglinton Avenue East, Suite 700, Toronto, Ontario, Canada M4P 2Y3
(a division of Pearson Penguin Canada Inc.)
Penguin Ireland, 25 St Stephen's Green, Dublin 2, Ireland
(a division of Penguin Books Ltd)
Penguin Group (Australia), 250 Camberwell Road, Camberwell, Victoria 3124, Australia
(a division of Pearson Australia Group Pty Ltd)
Penguin Books India Pvt Ltd, 11 Community Centre, Panchsheel Park, New Delhi – 110 017, India
Penguin Books (NZ), cnr Airborne and Rosedale Roads, Albany, Auckland 1310, New Zealand
(a division of Pearson New Zealand Ltd)
Penguin Books (South Africa) (Pty) Ltd, 24 Sturdee Avenue, Rosebank, Johannesburg 2196, South Africa

Penguin Books Ltd, Registered Offices: 80 Strand, London WC2R 0RL, England

www.penguin.com

This translation first published in Penguin Classics 2006
7

Translation and editorial material copyright © Bernard O'Donoghue, 2006
All rights reserved

The moral right of the translator has been asserted

Set in 10.25/12.25 pt PostScript Adobe Sabon
Typeset by Rowland Phototypesetting Ltd, Bury St Edmunds, Suffolk
Printed in England by Clays Ltd, St Ives plc

Except in the United States of America, this book is sold subject
to the condition that it shall not, by way of trade or otherwise, be lent,
re-sold, hired out, or otherwise circulated without the publisher's
prior consent in any form of binding or cover other than that in
which it is published and without a similar condition including this
condition being imposed on the subsequent purchaser

ISBN-13: 978-0-140-42453-9

www.greenpenguin.co.uk

Penguin Books is committed to a sustainable future
for our business, our readers and our planet.
The book in your hands is made from paper
certified by the Forest Stewardship Council.

Contents

Acknowledgements

I am very grateful to the staff of the Bodleian Library in Oxford and of the British Library. I first heard of the poem from my sister Eileen who pondered doing an M.A. on it at University College Cork in 1961. I first studied *Sir Gawain* with Christopher Ball and Nick Havely at Lincoln College, Oxford in the 1960s, and benefited greatly from the learning and humanity of them both. Since then I have learned most from many generations of students at Magdalen and Wadham Colleges, Oxford. They have assured me of the poem's enduring appeal. My version was scrutinized to its advantage by my wife, Heather, my daughter, Josie, and my incomparable copy-editor, Louisa Sladen. Above all this volume has been improved by the extraordinarily perceptive and logically alert reading by Hilary Laurie of Penguin Classics.

Introduction

It has often been said that *Sir Gawain and the Green Knight* (*c.* 1380) is one of the two great long poems in Middle English, the other being Geoffrey Chaucer's *Troilus and Criseyde* (*c.* 1385). Yet the experience of the two poems in the history of English literature could hardly be more different. Ever since his own writing lifetime in the last third of the fourteenth century, Chaucer has been a major, documented presence in that history. *Gawain* survived by chance, when many anonymous poems of the same kind did not, and was hardly mentioned – or read – until the nineteenth century when it was first printed. Yet its appeal for a modern readership is unfailing. The poem's voice, like the narrator's voice in Miguel Cervantes's *Don Quixote* (1605, 1615), is immediately recognizable to us: ironic, commonsensical and realistic.

How can such terms apply to a marginal poem by an unknown poet in Middle English, written in a language which is a great deal less familiar to us than Chaucer's? In many passages of the poem it is not an exaggeration to say that its language sounds wholly foreign to modern English speakers. For this reason, a readable modern English translation (and there are several of them already) is essential if we are to encounter the ironic common sense of the original poem. This is a pity, it must be conceded at once, because the graphic and fluent alliterative language of the original is one of its greatest strengths. For that reason I have put as an appendix here one of the most admired passages in the poem, with an analysis of the form of the original language.

THE MANUSCRIPT

The poem survives in a single manuscript, now held in the British Library, which has been dated to around 1400, the year of Chaucer's death. It is a small, unprepossessing manuscript book, written in a clear hand, in a language which is hard to place exactly, but which has usually been localized somewhere in the north-west English Midlands, on the borders of Staffordshire, Cheshire and Derbyshire. There are three other poems in the manuscript, in broadly the same language or dialect, and resembling *Gawain* in form to varying degrees. They are all much more evangelically Christian than *Gawain*, which is to say religious to an extent typical of many medieval Arthurian romances (some of which of course are very religious indeed). Of the other three poems, the most celebrated is the poetic elegy *Pearl*, the story of a dream-encounter between a narrating 'jeweller' and his lost pearl, which symbolizes a daughter who died at the age of two. The other two poems are Bible stories, also told in the brilliantly graphic language of the manuscript: *Patience*, the story of Jonah, in the whale and elsewhere, and *Cleanness* (which used to be called *Purity*, for alliterative classification with the other two), which is made up of versions of three biblical narratives. The most successful attempts to find common thematic elements have suggested that the poems are all concerned, more or less, with acceptance of the will of God by a protagonist who is initially resistant to it. All four poems have usually been taken as the work of a single poet, the 'Pearl'-poet or the 'Gawain'-poet, but there is no evidence for authorship, despite a number of attempts to find an author over the past fifty years. The strongest case for single authorship rests on a common dialect and a shared formal brilliance of language, far beyond the reach of most surviving contemporary poems. A fifth poem, not in the manuscript, is sometimes added to this putative corpus, *St Erkenwald*, written in the same dialect and about the miracles attending the exhumation of a Roman saint in London in the course of the building of St Paul's Cathedral.

THE POEM'S PLACE OF ORIGIN

It is always hard to say exactly where a poem like *Gawain*, from an outlying area of England and without a known date or author, comes from. In this case, there is clear evidence (in the way of textual corruption) that the dialect of the scribe is not exactly the same as the poet's. On the other hand, remarkably plausible efforts have been made to identify precisely two of the three central locales in the poem, the Green Chapel and Bertilak's castle. In particular, the work by R. W. V. Elliott in localizing the castle in the area around Leek in Staffordshire is enormously interesting.[1]

THE ATTRACTIONS OF *GAWAIN*

Whatever claims can be made for the other poems in the manuscript – and *Pearl* especially has always had enthusiastic advocates – it is *Sir Gawain and the Green Knight* that makes this group of poems a documentary survival of the first importance. So, while the likelihood that the unknown author of this brilliant romance was also the writer of a group of accomplished poetic narratives on biblical themes is highly significant, I will not discuss those other poems in detail. In *Gawain* the hero undergoes a set of experiences which, despite an incredibility acceptable in romance (he encounters a green man who can survive decapitation), have a remarkable psychological familiarity for us. The poem's modernity has been repeatedly acknowledged and reproduced. The story has frequently been retold for children; there is one remarkably effective film version (and one not so effective); there is a related novel *The Green Knight* by Iris Murdoch; and there is a superb opera by Harrison Birtwistle to a libretto by David Harsent.[2]

The story is well known so it can be told briefly. One New Year's Day, a day particularly devoted to festive celebration in late-medieval England, Arthur and the company of the Round Table are celebrating the season at Camelot when a huge, green knight – 'you'd think that he was some kind of half-giant' (l. 140) – rides into the hall on a green horse. He wants to make a deal: he will have his head cut off here and now with the axe he is carrying, on condition that his decapitator will come to his domicile, his 'Green Chapel', to have his head cut off in return in a year's time. Gawain takes on his challenge, and the Green Knight rides off, gruesomely holding his speaking head. At the end of the year Gawain sets off to keep the agreement, with no very clear idea where he is going, travelling on a northerly route through some familiar real places set in the romance environment. He spends the next Christmas period at a wonderful northern castle, where for three days the beautiful wife of the lord of the castle attempts to seduce him. Finally, he is directed to the Green Chapel, where he receives his fate at the hands of the Green Knight, and returns to Camelot to file his report, a sadder and wiser man.

Why is it so appealing, this story of Gawain, 'Mary's knight', who has taken a vow of chastity and who bears an image of the Blessed Virgin inside his shield, but makes an improbable pact of mutual decapitation – mutually assured destruction, it would seem? The rationale offered at the end – that the whole thing was conjured up by Arthur's malevolent half-sister Morgan Le Fay to scare his queen, Guinevere, her traditional enemy, to death – is flimsy in the extreme and, like the moral of many medieval poems, does not seem to meet the case. In several ways, the beauty is in the detail. The Vivaldi-like sequence of the seasons at the start of the second of the poem's four sections, before Gawain sets off to keep his bargain, is incomparably evoked, from the 'crabbed Lent' to the warm showers that make the birds hasten to build 'for solace of the soft summer', to the hardening harvest whose:

> ... dryness makes the dust swirl around
> and fling up high off the face of the earth. (ll. 523–4)

On his winter northward journey Gawain sleeps in his iron armour, nearly slain by the sleet, where the birds pipe piteously for pain of the cold. When he sees the castle that he thinks will be his salvation, it looks as if it is 'cut out of paper', like the French castles that illustrate fifteenth-century Books of Hours like that of the Duc de Berry (whose January miniature features a particularly *Gawain*-like New Year's feast). Perhaps as memorable and striking as anything for the blood-sickened reader in the twenty-first century is the panic of the wild animals as the hunt attacks them: 'They screamed and they bled and they died on the hills' (l. 1163).

But the distinction of the poem is far from confined to the observed minutiae. The writer's overall grasp of the narrative shows great imaginative control. Three pre-existing stories are woven together, as far as we know for the first time: the decapitation agreement; a familiar temptation scene in which a knight is amorously tempted by the wife of his host; and an 'exchange of winnings' in which two characters agree to exchange what they gain at the end of the day (or the ends of three consecutive days here). To link these separate stories together effectively would be impressive in itself; but in *Gawain* this linking is done with a clear, sustained purpose, to ask a question about romance and its often uncomplicated assumptions. The poem seems to ask (and the poem's best critic, John Burrow,[3] says the same kind of generically searching questions are asked by this writer's poetic contemporaries in the age of Richard II – Chaucer, Gower and Langland): what happens if the perfect knight, the hero of romance, has divided loyalties? He has to show perfect Christian chivalry, but also to be perfectly courteous to ladies; he has to be faithful to his word, but also to be uncompromising in action. How does Gawain square his necessity to be chaste with a courteous response to his temptress? How, at the end of each day, can he exchange the kisses he wins from her for her husband's winnings at hunting? And how above all can he, with his human, bodily frailty, face having his head cut off in exchange for the Green Knight's?

Another major critic of this poem, L. D. Benson,[4] called it 'a romance about romance'; that is to say, it is the very form, romance itself, that is being tested. It is being tested for its adequacy as a literary form: for its right to be taken seriously by a serious audience. The most miraculous achievement of the poem is that none of its elements is betrayed. Gawain may look foolish at the end, but the genre has survived. The qualities of romance, which Gawain possesses pre-eminently, are all shown to be worthwhile: courtesy, amorous language, religious fervour of course, generosity, love of fellow men, and – above all – fidelity to one's given word. Burrow says that, if the poem had a single-word title to bring it in line with the other poems in the manuscript, it would be 'truth', in the sense of fidelity.[5] *Sir Gawain and the Green Knight* shows above all, in the words of Chaucer's *The Franklin's Tale*, that 'Truth is the highest thing that man can keep'.

Between Tolkien and C. S. Lewis, from Borges to Eco, from *Montaillou* to Heaney's *Beowulf*, the Middle Ages have been much in vogue recently. Indeed, romance never lost its appeal after its revival in the nineteenth century. But the attractions of this poem are far beyond the popular, or beyond the romantic. Certainly it has noble and fearless knights, and beautiful, seductive ladies; it has magic and castles and threatening monsters (Ted Hughes's 'wodwos'), and marvels of all kinds. But its appeal has a sophistication and maturity well beyond such traditional romance trappings. The writer keeps us aware of this ambition to write something beyond the ordinary: at the beginning of the second of the poem's four sections, before Gawain sets off to meet his fate, we are warned that the outcome may be more serious than he has (or we have) bargained for. '[A] year passes quickly and changes its moods; the end rarely matches the spirit it starts in' (ll. 498–9). The poem presents us with classic romance travails and trials: seduction and physical threat. But – for the first time, it seems, in the annals of romance – it asks us to imagine what that is *really* like. You are tempted by your host's wife, as in several earlier romances, and now in the most compromising and attractive and explicit terms. How do you *really* feel? And, more importantly, how do you behave? Gawain is worried about his courtesy, 'lest crathayn he were' ('in case he'd seem boorish [towards the lady]', l. 1773), but he is more anxious not to 'betray that good lord whose castle it was' (l. 1775), her husband and his generous host, just as the morally responsible hero of a serious nineteenth-century novel would be. He is expressing the same concerns as Macbeth's duties of hospitality towards Duncan.

There are other aspects to this narrative that have an obvious modern appeal too. The first is its nature as a 'whodunnit'. It is as important reading *Gawain* not to know what is going to happen at the end as it is in a story by Poe or O. Henry or in a contemporary crime novel. The passage quoted in the previous paragraph makes this clear: it is indeed true of this poem that the state of things at the end is not the same as at the start. (As has also often been acknowledged, this makes it difficult to write an introduction without giving away some part of what the reader must not know until the end.) What is held back is not kept hidden *only* for suspense, however; it is integral to the serious meaning of this poem, which is finally serious to the point of life and death, despite its wonderful grace and lightness.

Such scruples are new in the romance. For as long as Tristan and Iseult, or Lancelot and Guinevere, could persuade the ladies' husbands that the evidence of adultery that they saw with their own eyes was false, neither they nor their stories were problematic. To be seen as guiltless was to be guiltless. But of course without those great adulterers, there would have been no supreme romances. The particular distinction of *Gawain* is to remain true to the spirit and narrative of such romance (it would be easy to dismiss that spirit as beneath serious or realistic consideration), while scrutinizing the form for its moral adequacy. If Gawain fails in the end, he fails in defence of the literary world he operates in.

And it is that world that triumphs at the end. It is not presented with the irony – however affectionate – of *Don Quixote*, even if the narrative voice occasionally recalls Cervantes's novel in its attitude to the hero. This is a seriously desirable and admirable world. The people in it are happy in the early Christmas scenes; it is a wonderful midwinter poem, celebrating the warmth of the indoors. The poem is of its age, but represents its age at its finest. And it succeeds by the finest poetic technique. The physical temptation of Gawain by the beautiful lady (the adjective is inadequate) is made real – we are returning to the minutiae after all – by the extraordinarily precise, tactile skills of the poetry. The mixture of erotic frisson and paralysed panic felt by Gawain when she suddenly sits on the edge of his bed is unsurpassed even in our age, which gives a lot of thought to such effects and fantasies. Sitting in her dêshabillé, described in insinuating detail, she tells Gawain 'Ye are welcum to my cors' (l. 1237). Some rather bowdlerizing attempts have been made to interpret this as a defused metaphor, meaning 'I welcome you', and it has been noted that it occurs in the less narratively significant rhyming 'wheel' (the four-line brief quatrain that occurs at the end of each more substantial stanza). But the fact remains that what she says, sitting on the edge of his bed, literally means 'You are welcome to my body'. Furthermore, this suggestive innuendo is totally in keeping with the lady's attitude throughout her three visits to Gawain's bedside, evoking states of mind with an exactness that seems astonishingly contemporary to us.

It is important to emphasize that this psychological naturalness is entirely in keeping with much of the literature of the high Middle Ages, with the European courtly love writings by the Provençal troubadours and the German Minnesänger of the period around 1200. There has been some rather pointless critical argument about whether Chaucer or the writer of *Gawain* is more 'English'. In some ways this poem is a particularly brilliant exercise in the principal genre of medieval literature, well beyond the compass of other writers of romance in England. But there seems something prophetic of the later English literary tradition in the pragmatic way that the poem refuses to leave unexamined the conventional *donnée* that a knight can be perfectly Christian and expert at love-talking at the same time. This practicality too is part of what the modern reader responds to in *Gawain*.

ANALOGUES, SOURCES AND TRADITION

The poem begins and ends with the idea of the 'Brut': that Britain, like Rome, was founded by Felix Brutus, a descendant of the Trojans after the fall of Troy. But this elegant framing has little to do with the substance of the story. *Gawain* is a new and complex romance that is made up of several familiar elements, such as the three stories I have mentioned already: the decapitation bargain, the exchange of winnings and the feminine temptation. Several parallels have been found for the decapitation contract, particularly the Irish Cuchulainn story *Fled Bricrend*,[6] and the originally Welsh story of Caradoc, perhaps known to this poet (who is clearly well read, on various evidence) as the *Livre de Caradoc*, a section of what is called the *First Continuation* of Chrétien de Troyes's *Perceval*, in which the attention shifts from Perceval to introduce a whole new Gawain romance.[7] Parallels for the temptation scenes are also very strong, especially the French romance *Le chevalier à l'epée* ('The Knight of the Sword', before 1210),[8] whose correspondences are stronger than has often been claimed. But in general it is not wise to tie down *Gawain* to particular influences, or to see it as a departure from a particular source, as has sometimes been done in relation to the *Fled Bricrend*. None of the story elements is very unexpected in the romance world; it is their intricate joining together by this poet which is so remarkable (the kind of literary conjoining that medieval commentators called 'antancion' or 'conjunctura'). Like Chaucer and Shakespeare, this medieval romance writer did not make up stories or adapt existing single narratives in any simple way.

Apart from the poem's clear relations in the world of romance, one other set of cultural relations has been suggested for *Gawain*, in a series of interpretations that were collectively dismissed by C. S. Lewis and others as 'the anthropological approach'. An extreme version of this was proposed by John Spiers,[9] who saw the poem's more profound meaning to lie in its links with the natural world's yearly cycle, connected with such seasonal things as mummers' plays, in which allegorical figures acted out the events associated with the changing seasons. Interpretations along these lines were founded in such canonical works as Robert Graves's *The White Goddess*, which suggested that the deeper meanings of literary works with links to a folk tradition, as romances have, are to be sought at a subliminal, sub-textual level. The Green Knight as a midwinter vegetation figure, it is suggested, somehow links with Gawain as a sun god (Gawain did have some such associations with an earlier avatar, the Welsh semi-divinity Gwalchmei),[10] and the story in the poem connects with the killing of the old year and the revival of the new. Some of the most appealing things in the poem link to the seasons and the life principle: in the great passage describing the stages of the year when Gawain is setting off on his quest, the autumn warns the grain to harden before the trials of winter; at the end, Gawain's attachment to his life wins him the Green Knight's approval. But such links, suggestive though they are, have little to do with the concerns or appeal of the poem as it stands, even if such vestiges feed an important vein of life in the poem. *Gawain* is as independent of those distant sources as of its more proximate ones. Although operating with paralleled story elements, and keeping faithful to the spirit of the romance world, it stands outside its traditions as a work of imaginative originality that speaks to all ages.

NOTES

1. R. W. V. Elliott, *The 'Gawain' Country* (Leeds, 1984), and especially 'Landscape and Geography' in the most valuable collection of essays on this poem and the others in the manuscript *A Companion to the 'Gawain'-Poet*, edited by Derek Brewer and Jonathan Gibson (Cambridge, 1997), pp. 103–17.
2. For a good summary of modern versions, see Barry Windeatt and David J. Williams in Brewer and Gibson, *Companion*.
3. J. A. Burrow, *Ricardian Poetry* (London, 1971).
4. L. D. Benson, *Art and Tradition in 'Sir Gawain and the Green Knight'* (New Brunswick, 1965).
5. J. A. Burrow, *A Reading of Sir Gawain and the Green Knight* (London, 1965), p. 25.
6. G. Henderson (ed. and trans.), *Fled Bricrend: Bricriu's Feast* (London, 1899).
7. For an excellent detailed account and translated texts of some important sources and analogues of *Gawain*, see L. E. Brewer, *'Sir Gawain and the Green Knight': Sources and Analogues*,

Arthurian Studies 27, 2nd edn (Woodbridge, 1992), and the same writer's chapter 'The Sources of *Sir Gawain*' in Brewer and Gibson, *Companion*, pp. 243–55. The *First Continuation of Perceval* was edited by W. Roach (Philadelphia, 1949); see p. xiii for parallels with *Sir Gawain and the Green Knight*.

8. L. E. Brewer, *'Sir Gawain and the Green Knight': Sources and Analogues*, pp. 109ff.
9. John Spiers, *Medieval English Poetry, The Non-Chaucerian Tradition* (London, 1952), pp. 215ff.
10. Described by R. S. Loomis in *Arthurian Tradition and Chrétien de Troyes* (New York, 1949), pp. 146–8.

Further Reading

The four poems in the manuscript (British Library MS. Cotton Nero A.x) were reproduced in facsimile for the Early English Text Society with an introduction by I. Gollancz (Oxford, 1923). To read the poem in the original without full-scale study of its rich and eccentric Middle English poetic language, there are two possible short cuts. First, there are a number of parallel-text versions, of which the most useful is W. R. J. Barron's prose translation, facing a text based on the EETS facsimile of the manuscript (Manchester, 1974). A second relatively painless way of reading the original is in the Everyman edition, first edited by A. C. Cawley (1962), and revised by J. J. Anderson, *Sir Gawain and the Green Knight, Pearl, Cleanness, Patience* (London, 1996), which glosses obscure words to the side of the text and translates difficult lines at the foot of the page. The standard scholarly edition is Norman Davis's 1967 second edition of J. R. R. Tolkien and E. V. Gordon's 1925 Oxford edition. Davis's good glossary and notes can be supplemented by those in Theodore Silverstein's edition (Chicago, 1984). The best overall critical study of the poem remains J. A. Burrow's *A Reading of Sir Gawain and the Green Knight* (London, 1965). The most valuable handbook for all contextual matters is Derek Brewer and Jonathan Gibson (eds.), *A Companion to the 'Gawain'-Poet* (Cambridge, 1997). A useful compendium of analogical material and sources is L. E. Brewer (ed.), *'Sir Gawain and the Green Knight': Sources and Analogues*, 2nd edn (Woodbridge, 1992). Readers who are interested in the general development of any Arthurian text from Celtic origins onwards should turn to R. S. Loomis's magisterial *Arthurian Literature in the Middle Ages: A Collaborative History* (Oxford, 1959). A detailed and exhaustive study of the poem's poetic language is Marie Borroff, *Sir Gawain and the Green Knight: A Stylistic and Metrical Study* (New Haven, 1962). Among previous translations, Tolkien's and Borroff's both attempt to reflect the stylistic structure of the original in their renderings.

A Note on the Translation

All great poetry is untranslatable, and this is perhaps particularly true of writing like the 'Gawain'-poet's, which is formally so highly wrought. As illustrated by the passage of the original included as the Appendix here, the long lines of the original are principally characterized by a ringing consonantal alliteration. As most previous translators have agreed, it is not possible to sustain this alliterative pattern – with three or more alliterating consonants in every line – without losing the precise meaning in modern English and without sacrificing any claim to idiomatic naturalness. A highly 'poetic' translation can opt to do this: the most famously successful instance is Ezra Pound's version of the Anglo-Saxon poem *The Seafarer*. But in my translation I am aiming at plain style modern verse, comparable, say, to Thomas Kinsella's style in representing the medieval Irish of *The Táin* (from a literary tradition with which *Gawain* has things in common).

To explain why this seems to me the best strategy, we may recall the poetic tradition that *Gawain* belongs to. It is one of the principal texts of the 'Alliterative Revival', a movement in late Middle English which either revived, or adopted as a stylistic antiquarianism, the formal practices of Old English verse, rather than the European system of rhyming syllabic lines favoured by Chaucer and his successors. This was based on rhythmic patterns rather than the foot- and syllable-counting of iambic pentameter. It is sometimes claimed that it is a more natural form in English than the iambic pattern which has dominated English verse since Shakespeare.

The rhythmic alliterative line was divided into two halves,

each containing two (or in the first half-line occasionally three) main stresses. In Old English the alliteration followed an invariable pattern across the line, which can be written *aa/ax*. That is to say, the significant alliteration occurs on the initial syllables in the first three stresses of the line and never in the fourth. To put it another way: the third stress (that is, the first stress of the second half-line) always alliterates with one or both of the stresses in the first half-line, but never with the fourth stress. Lines 3 and 4 of *Gawain* follow this pattern:

Þe tulk þat þe trammes of tresoun þer wroȝt
watȝ tried for his tricherie, Þe trewest on erthe

(In a literal prose translation: 'The man who performed the machinations of treason there / Was tried for (or 'known for') his treachery, the most certain in the world'.) Many modern translations have attempted to reproduce some parts of this system – in some cases (such as Borroff's version in 1967) with impressive success. But it is impossible to reproduce these formalities in anything like normal modern English, without introducing anachronisms of vocabulary or word order. Borroff's version of the two lines I have quoted is:

The knight that had knotted the nets of deceit
Was impeached for his perfidy, proven most true,

correctly alliterating on the first three main stresses and not the fourth. In my version I have abandoned alliteration altogether, while keeping firmly to what seems to me to be the original stress-pattern as it survives into modern English:

the man who'd betrayed it was brought to trial,
most certainly guilty of terrible crimes.

My aim has been to keep strictly to the rhythm of the original, while replacing the phonetic formalities (alliteration most importantly) with the normal formalities of modern English. In practice this has meant that I have often (as here) moved towards the ten- or eleven-syllable line of post-Shakespearean blank verse, even if this has not been a conscious intention.

There is a further major formal matter to be addressed by the translator of *Gawain*. A glance at the pages of even a translated version like this will show how the long-lined stanzas of unequal length in the poem end with a device which has been called the 'bob and wheel', a short phrase of two words containing one stress, the bob, followed by a four-line rhyming quatrain made up of three-stressed lines (rhyming iambic trimeters). Most previous translators have chosen, for good reasons, to accentuate the extreme formal departure from the main stanzas in these sections by keeping at least the half-rhyme in the second and fourth lines of these 'wheel' quatrains. I have chosen not to: it seems to me no less essential to maintain the modern plain style in these shorter sections as in the main stanzas. The crucial change of pace they effect to break up the narrative is evident from a glance at their shape on the page, making it unnecessary to treat their lexical or prosodic make-up differently from the rest.

Vocabulary is another vital element in the distinction of this great poem. Chaucer's language is a heroic weaving together of several kinds of language: romance vocabulary from French side by side with plain Old English; Latinate high style alongside satirically reductive everyday language. But the language of *Gawain* and the other poems in its manuscript is much more diverse and inventive. This is another element in its untranslatability. Many of the terms in *Gawain* – from Old English and Norse, for example – are at least partly a product of its provenance in the north-west Midlands. But they are just as much a product of its alliterative and descriptive demands. To take as an example one of the poem's most memorable lines, describing the grim adversary that Gawain will have to face:

> Hym think as queme hym to quelle as quyk go hymselven
> (l. 2109)

This translates literally 'it is as pleasing to him to kill people as to be alive himself'. This loses entirely the Old English alliterating trio 'cweme', 'cwellan' and 'cwic': 'pleasing', 'kill', and 'alive'. But there is nothing to be done about it in a modern version that resists a 'translatorese' descent into non-modern idiom. My version here –

> He is as pleased to kill others as to have life himself –

loses everything apart from a consistent forward narrative drive and consistency of language.

There are more complex formal effects in the poem's language which I have also not attempted to reproduce. These are described fully in a brilliant analysis by Marie Borroff, *Sir Gawain and the Green Knight: A Stylistic and Metrical Study* (New Haven, 1962). Borroff shows, for example, that there is a tendency for colloquial terminology to occur in the unalliterating stress at the end of the line. Silverstein's edition shows that the language of the original habitually draws on stylistic effects taken from classical and medieval handbooks of rhetoric. The most crucial loss in a modernizing translation is of the distinctions in register of its vocabulary, between the poetic and the colloquial (the range of terms for 'man' is a notorious example), which are impossible to reproduce in intelligible modern English prose.

Nevertheless, I believe the greatest strength of this poem's language, and the strength I have tried not to lose, is the feature that has been found appealing in native Middle English (and in Old English) by poets from Hopkins to Auden to Heaney. Various terms have been used for this kind of metre which depends on stress rather than syllable- or foot-counting: Hopkins's 'sprung rhythm' is a particularly felicitous phrase for it. Accordingly, the only constraint that I have consistently imposed here, apart from keeping my version almost invariably line for line with the original, is the requirement of four stresses in each line of the stanza and three stresses in each line of the rhyming wheel. The poet of the original imposed these too, as well as many others, especially alliteration.

But what is most remarkable about *Gawain*, in metre as in genre, is the way constraints are mixed with freedoms. The alliteration and the stress pattern are demanding; so is the pattern of numerology which underlies the poem in some way which it is now difficult to spell out fully. (The two central episodes of the poem are a year and a day apart, corresponding to a familiar romance motif; *Pearl* is 1,212 lines and 101 stanzas long – a length which requires the addition of an asymmetrical extra stanza in one of the poem's sections. It seems probable that *Gawain*, which also has 101 stanzas and extends to just beyond 2,525 lines, was meant to – or originally did – conform to a similar numerological frame.) But side by side with these exacting formal requirements, *Gawain* – unlike *Pearl* – allows itself unusual formal freedoms. For example, the line lengths vary enormously, as a glance at any page will again illustrate; so does the stanza length, extending from thirteen lines to thirty-seven. Such is the variation in stanza length, indeed, that it might be more accurate to describe the poem as not stanzaic at all but as a continuous narrative (as many romances were), broken up at irregular intervals by bob and wheels. The poem conforms to the aesthetic principle of regularity within irregularity to a remarkable degree. And it is that principle that I have tried to stay faithful to, as well as to the lexicon and idiom of modern English.

A Note on the Text

Sir Gawain and the Green Knight was first edited by Sir Frederic Madden in 1839, and by now there are a great number of modern editions, all drawing on the sole medieval manuscript. There are places where that manuscript has clearly made mistakes; in some cases there is not universal agreement about how those mistakes are to be rectified. Like most editors, I have looked at the manuscript as well as consulting several modern editions (although Norman Davis's 1967 edition remains the most cited, some of its readings have by now been superseded by the editions by Silverstein, Burrow, Barron and others, listed in the Further Reading). In the few cases where my translation depends on an unusual reading, I have indicated that in a note (at line 157, for instance). Most of my annotations, however, are intended to clarify references in the original text, rather than particular readings.

Sir Gawain and the Green Knight

I

When the war and the siege of Troy were all over
and the city flattened to smoking rubble,
the man who'd betrayed it was brought to trial,
most certainly guilty of terrible crimes.
Then the noble Aeneas and his royal line
swept across Europe and lived as the rulers
of every country in the western world.
Powerful Romulus settled at Rome
and founded that city of greatest distinction.
He gave it his name, which is what it's still known by. 10
Ticius made his base in the blue Tuscan hills
and Langobard his on Lombardy's plains.
But over the Channel, illustrious Brutus
colonized Britain and its rolling mountains
to his great content.
War, reprisal, exploit
have happened here at times.
Joy and disaster
have often taken turns.

After Britain was founded by this powerful leader, 20
brave people were bred there with a liking for warfare,
who chose to do battle in turbulent times.
More marvels too have occurred in our land
than anywhere else since the fall of Troy.
Of all that ruled here as kings of the Britons
the noblest was Arthur, by every account.
So my purpose is now to describe an adventure,

which people agree was clearly an event
extraordinary even by the standards of Arthur.
30 If you'll pay attention for just a short while
I'll tell it straight, just as I heard it,
word for word,
exactly as passed down
in every detail,
by each generation
down all the days.

It was Christmas at Camelot, and there was the king
with his leading lords and all his best soldiers,
the famous company of the whole Round Table –
40 celebrating in style: not a care in the world.
Again and again strong men tussled,
and the noble knights jousted with vigour
till they rode to the court to start on the dancing.
Celebrations continued the whole of a fortnight
with all the feasting and pleasure that people could
think of.
It was fine to hear such glorious commotion:
lively uproar all day and dancing at night,
the sheerest indulgence in dance hall and bedroom
by the ladies and lords, whatever whim took them.
50 With all worldly pleasures they dwelt there together:
the most famous knights in the annals of Christendom,
the prettiest women that ever drew breath,
and the handsomest king at the head of them all.
For these were people in the flower of life,
in that hall.
Most successful in the world,
their king held full control.
It would be hard nowadays
to find such fellowship.

60 With the change of the calendar on New Year's Day
the courses were doubled for the top table.
When the king and the knights arrived in the hall

and Mass was over in the echoing chapel,
the singing continued from priests and the rest,
and 'Noel!' was called out over and over.
Then out they ran to bring in the presents,
and, shouting greetings, they handed them round,
excitedly arguing which were the best.
Ladies laughed outright when asked to pay up,
the men who won favours were hardly complaining, 70
and all this cavorting went on until mealtime.
When they'd dressed for dinner they took their places,
the nobler the higher, in proper degree.
Guinevere the queen was set in the middle,
elegantly dressed on her rich throne,
cushioned in silks beneath her red canopy
and, hanging around her, Tharsian drapes,
embroidered and studded with the finest gems
that money could buy at the highest price
at the time. 80
Too beautiful to describe
her grey eyes shone.
No one could ever say
they had seen a greater beauty.

But Arthur would not eat until everyone was served,
he was so young and impulsive – you might call him
boyish.
He liked life eventful and he couldn't bear
to lie late in bed or to sit down for long,
so much his young blood and active brain roused him.
He had another ritual he kept to as well 90
on such major feasts: by tradition
he would never sit and eat before someone told him
a new story of some great adventure,
some major marvel he could fully believe in,
about princes or armed feats or other great deeds;
or else until someone asked for a knight
to fight against, to risk life in combat,
man against man and life against life,

to see which of them fortune would favour.
100 This was the king's humour when he was in court
with his gracious company at every grand feast
in the hall.
So with proud bearing
he stood there in his place.
Full of life at New Year
he was cheerful with them all.

So there he stood, the powerful king
before the high table, making graceful small talk.
Noble Sir Gawain sat next to the queen
110 and Agravain the Hardhand on her other side,
both the king's nephews and trustworthy knights.
Bishop Baldwin was at the head of the table,
and Ywain, son of Urien, sat by his side.
Set at the top, these were served with honour,
and then all the knights along the side tables.
In came the first course, to the pealing of trumpets
that had brilliant banners hanging beneath them.
The beating of drums and the noble pipes
with their martial music awakened the echoes,
120 so that every heart leapt, aroused by the sound.
Delicacies were brought of the rarest foods
in endless abundance, on plates of such number
it was hard to find room in front of the diners
to set down the silver that held all these dishes
there on the cloth.
No one stinted them
as they all helped themselves.
Twelve dishes to each couple,
good beer and gleaming wine.

130 I'll give no more details about this rich feast;
you'll have got the idea, that there was no shortage.
But suddenly a strange noise came to their ears,
which might free the king to sit down to the table.
Hardly had the clatter of plates died down

and the first course been duly served to the court
when a monstrous apparition strode in the door,
one of the tallest creatures in the whole of the earth.
So square and powerful from neck to waist,
his thighs and his forearms so muscly and long
you'd think that he was some kind of half-giant. 140
But I think what he was was the hugest of men,
the most pleased with his size of anyone living.
For, though his back and his chest were incredibly big,
his stomach and waist were fashionably trim,
and all his features in proportion, given his size,
exactly right.
They were shocked by his colour though,
apparent at first glance;
what was most uncanny was
he was *green* from head to toe! 150

This man and his clothes were all coloured green.
He'd a tight-fitting coat, well made for his size.
Over it he wore an elegant cloak,
lined with bleached fur, and the braid was edged
with the richest ermine: the same with his hood,
which was off his head and draped on his shoulders.
Neat, tight stockings of the same colour
clung to his calves; his polished spurs
were gleaming gold, shining on silk,
and his feet stood shoeless on the stirrups. 160
And all his attire was totally green,
to the stripes on his belt and the various gems
that were lavishly studded on every part,
on a background of silk, on saddle and tunic.
It would be too much to list half the adornments
stitched on his clothes, the birds and the insects,
all splashes of bright green set against gold.
All the horse's tackling – the rich crupper,
the bosses on the bit – was enamelled metal:
the stirrups he stood on embellished the same way, 170
saddle-bows too, and the regal horse-cloths

that shone and sparkled with their green jewels.
The horse he was mounted on exactly the same,
in every detail.
A green horse: strong, well set,
a steed hard to hold back,
but by the embroidered reins
responsive to his rider.

This man was a picture, dressed in green as he was,
180 and the mane of his horse an identical colour.
Luxuriant hair wrapped round his shoulders;
a huge beard like a bush hung over his chest,
matching the long hair that flowed from his head,
cut all round just over the elbows
so that half of his arms were wreathed round by it,
like the cloak of a king closed in at the neck.
The mane of the big horse was cropped the same way:
waved and curled, with rich ringlets
woven with gold thread into the green hair,
190 one strand of hair, then one strand of gold.
His tail and his forelock were plaited the same,
and each bound up with a ribbon of green.
The docked tail had gems the whole of its length,
and was tied at the top with an intricate knot,
where many gold-burnished bells rang out.
A horse of such a kind, or such a man astride it,
they had never seen in that hall before,
with human eyes.
He looked as fast as lightning,
200 so all that saw him said.
It seemed as if no man
could survive beneath his blows.

But he was wearing neither helmet nor mail coat,
nor any breastplate or armour at all,
neither spear nor shield to thrust or to strike.
But in one hand he had a bough of holly,
the greenest tree when groves are bare,

and an axe in the other, outlandishly big,
too cruel a weapon for words to describe.
The huge head was a metre in length, 210
the blade of fresh steel and coloured gold;
the edge shone brightly and the broad blade
was as well honed to cut as the sharpest razor.
The shaft the man gripped it by was made of hard
wood,
reinforced with iron right to the end
and all engraved with skilled work in green.
A cord was wrapped round it, tied at the head,
crossed over all the length of the handle
with many precious tassels fixed along it,
twisted tightly on to green buttons. 220
This knight rode in, right into the hall
and strode up to the dais, fearful of nothing.
He acknowledged no one but looked over their heads,
and the first thing he said was, 'Where
is the noblest of all of this crowd? I'd like to speak
to him in particular, to exchange some words
politely.'
He looked at all the knights,
glancing up and down;
then stopped to consider 230
who had most honour there.

They all gazed and gazed upon this green stranger,
because everyone wondered what it could mean
that a rider and horse might be such a colour –
green as grass, and greener it seemed
than green enamel glowing bright against gold.
They all stood wondering, then crept a bit closer,
transfixed with wonder as to what he would do.
They had seen many marvels but nothing like this,
so they assumed it must be magic and witchcraft. 240
Most noble knights were afraid to respond,
so stunned by his voice that they stayed there
stock-still

in an eerie silence which filled the great hall.
Their voices were as silent as if they had fallen
asleep.
I think not all from fear
but partly through courtesy,
they left it to the king
to make some response.

250 When Arthur from the dais saw all that was happening,
he greeted him at once – he was fearful of nothing.
He said, 'Sir, you are welcome indeed to this place.
I am Arthur, the head of the house.
Please dismount, and stay, I beg you,
and later we will learn what your pleasure might be.'
'By the high Lord of heaven,' he answered, 'no, thank
you.
I have not come to linger here long,
but because your praises so highly are sung, Sir,
and because your knights are reputed the best
260 and the strongest in arms of riders on horseback,
most brave and most worthy of all humankind,
valiant to engage with in all noble sports.
Here is shown chivalry, or so I am told,
and it is simply that which brings me here now.
But be reassured by this branch that I carry
that I come here in peace, not looking for strife.
If I had come in war with violent intentions,
I've got armour at home, and a helmet as well,
a shield and sharp spear, both shining bright,
270 and other weapons to wield, I assure you of that.
But I don't want battle; my dress is for peace.
If you are as brave as everyone says
you will generously grant me the exchange I ask for
as a right.'
Arthur answered, saying,
'Most gracious Sir,
if you want single combat
you will not lack it here.'

'No, I don't want a fight, I swear in all honesty.
On those benches they are mere adolescents. 280
If I were fully armed on my powerful horse,
there's no one to match me here, so small is their
strength.
All I ask in this court is one Christmas game,
at this New Year holiday with young people all round.
If any in this company thinks himself brave,
so hot in his blood and so wild in his head
that he dare give a stroke in exchange for another,
I'll make him a present of this handsome weapon,
this weighty axe to wield as he wants to,
and I'll take the first blow, as I stand here,
defenceless. 290
If anyone's so warlike as to give what I ask for,
to come up here and take over this weapon,
I relinquish it for good: he can call it his own.
I will stand for his blow, unflinching on this floor,
provided you agree I may give a stroke
in return.
I will give him a respite
of one year and a day.
Now come on; let's find out
if anyone dares to speak.' 300

If they were astonished at first, they grew even more
silent,
all the warriors in the hall, the greater and lesser.
The man on horseback turned in the saddle
and scarily glared round with his red eyes,
furrowed his bristling brows, shining green,
his beard sweeping all directions, to see who'd stand up.
When no one responded he snorted aloud,
drew himself up, and launched into speech.
'Well!' said the knight, 'so this is Arthur's court,
whose fame spreads wide through so many
kingdoms. 310
Where is your pride now? Where are your conquests,

your battles and fierceness and your big words?
It seems the Round Table's fame and celebrity
are banished with a word from one man's voice,
since all of you tremble before a blow has been struck!'
And he laughed so loud that the king was outraged.
For shame the blood rushed up to his cheeks
        and noble face.
    He grew as angry as the wind;
320 they all did who were there.
    The king, so brave by nature,
    stepped to the huge knight's side,

and said, 'Sir, for God's sake, your request is foolish;
but, if that's what you want, it's right you should get it.
I know of no one who fears your big words.
Now give me your axe, for the love of God,
and I will grant you the favour you ask for.'
He quickly jumped across and reached for his hand,
and the other man dismounted aggressively.
330 Arthur held his axe, gripped the handle,
and swung it round grimly, as if meaning to strike.
The powerful man towered above him,
taller than anyone there by a head and more.
With full self-assurance he stood stroking his beard,
till with a calm face he drew down his tunic,
no more frightened of Arthur's great threats
than if it was someone offering him
        a glass of wine.
    Gawain, next to the queen,
340 leaned over towards the king.
    'I beg you, most fervently,
    to let me take this on.

'If you, noble lord,' said Gawain to the king,
'let me rise from this bench and stand with you there,
to move from this table without giving offence,
if there's no objection from my lady the queen,
I'll take over from you before all the court.

For I think it unfitting, as is surely the case,
when this arrogant request is made in your hall,
that you should feel moved to meet it yourself, 350
while so many brave knights are sitting all round you
than whom no men on earth are more ready and willing
nor abler in body when battle begins.
I'm the weakest, I know, and the feeblest of spirit,
so my life would be the least loss, it is simply true.
My only worth is that you are my uncle;
my body's sole value that your blood runs through it.
Since this crazy task is not fitting for you,
and since I asked for it first, you should pass it to me.
If I speak out of turn, then don't let this court 360
be blamed.'
The noble knights consulted,
and all advised the same:
to exempt the royal king
and give Gawain the task.

Then the king commanded his knight to stand,
and he rose up at once, acting most properly.
He knelt before the king and took hold of the weapon.
Arthur yielded it freely, raised up his hand
and gave Gawain God's blessing, urging him 370
that his heart should be resolute, and his hand should
too.
'Be sure, cousin,' the king said, 'to make your cut right.
If you do it effectively, I believe for sure
that you can wait without worry for the blow he gives
you.'
Gawain went to the knight with the axe in his hand
and squarely awaited him, in no way afraid.
Then the knight in green addressed Sir Gawain.
'We must recap our terms before we go further.
But first let me ask you to tell me your name.
Tell me honestly so I can believe you.' 380
'Truly,' said the good knight, 'I am called Gawain,
I who offer you this blow, whatever comes after.

Twelve months from now I'll take one from you
with what weapon you choose, and from nobody else
alive.'
The other man answered,
'Sir Gawain, by my life I swear
I am entirely happy
that you should strike this blow.

390 'By God, Sir Gawain,' the Green Knight then said,
'I'm glad it's from your hands I'm to get what I asked.
And you've rightly described, in every detail,
the full exchange that I asked of the king,
except to assure me on your word of honour
that you will seek me yourself, wherever you think
I may be found on the earth, and take repayment
of what you give me today before this assembly.'
'But where must I look?' said Gawain. 'Where do you
live?
I swear by my maker, I have no notion,
400 and I don't know either your court or your name.
But give me directions, and say what you are called,
and I'll do my best to make my way there.
I solemnly swear it, on my word of honour.'
'That's enough this New Year, there's no more to be
said,'
said the knight in green to the noble Gawain.
'If I tell you it all when I've taken the blow
and you've struck me as agreed – if I tell you then
of my house and my home and what my name is,
then you can keep our agreement by feeling my strength.
410 And if I say nothing, then so much the better
for you: stay at home and look no further –
But enough!
Now take up your grim weapon
and let's see how you strike.'
'With pleasure, Sir,' said Gawain,
weighing his axe.

The Green Knight then duly took up his position,
and bent his head down a bit, exposing the skin.
His luxuriant hair he drew over his head,
to leave his neck exposed to view. 420
Gawain gripped his axe and lifted it up,
his left foot forward, square on the ground,
and dropped the blade swiftly on the unguarded skin
so that the warrior's weapon shattered the bones
and cut through the flesh, severing it completely
so the shining edge bit into the floor.
The handsome head fell from the neck to the ground
and several of them kicked it away as it rolled.
Blood gushed from the body and shone red against
green.
And yet the man neither staggered nor fell, 430
but, stepping out strongly on his vigorous legs,
to their horror reached out to where the knights
stood,
took hold of his beautiful head and lifted it up.
Then he turned to his horse and seized the reins,
stepped on the stirrups and leaped on its back,
holding his head by the hair with his hand.
He sat in the saddle just as securely
as if nothing had happened to him, headless
though he was.
He swung his body round, 440
a disfigured, bleeding trunk.
Many there were shaking
by the time he'd finished speaking.

He held the head up straight with his hand,
and turned the face towards the king who sat on the
throne.
He raised his eyelids and stared at him open-eyed;
then with his mouth said the words you will hear.
'Be sure, Gawain, you're ready, as you have sworn
to seek conscientiously until you find me,
as you've said in this hall, in these knights' hearing. 450

Seek out the Green Chapel, I urge you, to get
such a blow as you have struck. You've earned the right
to be promptly repaid on New Year's morning.
Most people call me the Green Chapel Knight;
so, if you ask, you won't fail to find me.
Therefore come, or be called a defaulter.'
With a violent tug he pulled the reins round,
and galloped out the hall door, his head in his hand,
so that fire from the flint sparked off the hooves.
460 To what country he went no one there knew,
any more than they knew where he'd come from at first.
What next?
The king and Gawain then
laughed at this green man.
But they had to face the truth
that it was unnatural.

If the noble King Arthur was uncertain at heart,
he didn't let it show, but with a brave voice
spoke to the queen in delicate words.
470 'My dear wife, do not be dismayed.
Such activities are fitting at Christmas –
playing of games, laughter and singing,
with the seasonal dancing of ladies and knights.
In any case, I can eat with a good conscience;
I can hardly deny that I have seen a marvel.'
He gazed then at Gawain and addressed him directly.
'Now, Sir, hang up your axe; it has done enough
hewing.'
So it was placed above the throne against the wall-
hangings,
where everyone could view it as a wonder
480 and tell of those marvels by pointing it out.
Then they turned to the table, the two of them together,
the king and the great knight who were rapidly served
double measures of everything, as befits the most noble.
With all kinds of food to accompanying music

they spent the day in enjoyment, until it ended
all over the world.
Now take care, Sir Gawain,
not to shrink from danger.
This is quite an ordeal
that you have taken on. 490

II

This adventure was a fine New Year's gift
for Arthur to get, for he loved to have challenges.
If topics were lacking when they sat to the table,
now they'd much deadly matter to keep their tongues
busy.
Gawain was pleased that he'd started these hall games,
but don't be surprised if the outcome is tragic.
Though people are cheerful when they've all been
drinking,
a year passes quickly and changes its moods;
the end rarely matches the spirit it starts in.
500 Yuletide is past and the New Year is too,
and each season follows the other in sequence.
After Christmas comes shrivelling Lent
that tries the body with fish and dry bread.
Then the earth's weather weakens the winter:
the cold shrinks underground, the clouds draw up
higher.
The bright rain falls in warming showers,
straight on to the ground so that flowers appear.
Both meadows and fields are covered in green;
birds hurry to build and sing with excitement
510 out of joy at the summer that follows so sweetly
all over the hills.
Blossoms swell and bloom
in dense, reckless array,
and rich notes, unpausing,
are heard throughout the wood.

After the soft breeze of the summer season
and the west wind that fans seeds and grasses,
the growth is abundant that issues all round,
when the soaking dew drops off the leaves
with the touch of heaven that the warm sun brings. 520
But then comes autumn to harden the grain,
to warn it to ripen ahead of the winter.
Its dryness makes the dust swirl around
and fling up high off the face of the earth.
The rough wind in the sky wrestles with the sun;
the lime-tree leaves loosen and fall to the ground,
and the grass turns grey that had just been so green.
All ripens, then rots, that sprang in such hope.
So the year passes on through its series of yesterdays,
and winter comes round again, as nature demands, 530
ever the same.
The moon around Michaelmas
has a touch of winter to it,
and Gawain thinks again
about his fearful quest.

Yet until All Saints' Day he stayed on with Arthur,
who held a feast on that festival in honour of Gawain,
with great celebration by all the Round Table.
Fine knights and beautiful ladies
were filled with despair for the sake of this man, 540
but yet they displayed nothing but gaiety:
many who grieved for him were still making jokes.
After dinner he spoke seriously to Arthur
and talked of his journey, openly saying,
'Now, lord of my life, I ask leave to depart.
You know how grave this adventure will be;
to speak more of its pains would be wasted breath.
But tomorrow I must set off to receive that blow,
to seek out that creature in green, God help me!'
Then the best of the company crowded together: 550
Iwain and Erec and many another,
Sir Dodinel the Wild, the Duke of Clarence,

Lancelot and Lionel, the noble Lucan,
Sir Bors and Sir Bedivere, both big men,
and other famous knights, such as Mador de la Port.
All this great company drew near to the king
to advise Gawain with heavy hearts.
Much deep sorrow was felt in the hall,
that one as valued as him should go on this quest,
560 to suffer a dire blow, unable to hit back
with his sword.
The knight still kept cheerful
and said, 'Why should I despair?
With destiny, good or bad,
you can only take your chance.'

He stayed all that day, and early next morning
asked for his armour, which duly was brought.
First an opulent carpet was laid on the floor,
and the rich golden armour spread out upon it.
570 The brave man stepped forward and handled the steel.
He was dressed in a tunic of rich Tharsian silk
and a finely cut cloak, buttoned to the neck
and trimmed on the inside with pure white fur.
Then they set armed shoes on his feet,
covered his legs in handsome steel greaves
with hinges attached, polished bright
and tied round the knees with knots of gold.
Fine thigh-sections elegantly encased
his strong muscular limbs, fastened with leather.
580 Last, the ornate armour of bright steel rings
wrapped around the knight's proud clothes,
with polished arm-pieces on both sides,
elegant elbow-guards and gloves of steel plate:
all fine chainmail to stand him in good stead
in his peril:
a fine suit of armour,
gold spurs tied with care
and a trustworthy sword,
hanging by the finest silk.

When he was fully dressed, his armour was lordly, 590
the least link or knot shining with gold.
Thus, armed as he was, he went to hear Mass,
celebrated solemnly at the high altar.
Then he went to the king and his court companions,
and took fond farewells of the lords and the ladies,
who escorted him with a kiss, praying for him to Christ.
Then Gryngolet was prepared, fitted with a saddle
that gleamed brightly with a line of gold fringes,
newly harnessed all over, ready for the road.
The bridle was plaited with the brightest gold, 600
and the ornate side-skirts and rich chest-trappings,
crupper and horse-cloth matched the saddle-bows.
It was all fastened with light red-gold nails
that shone and sparkled like the beams of the sun.
Then Gawain fervently kissed his helmet,
which was strongly forged and padded inside.
It stood high on his head, clasped at the back,
with a light silk band across the neck-guard,
picked out and encircled with the finest gems
on its broad silk edges, with birds such as parrots 610
embroidered on the seams amid periwinkles
and turtle-doves and love-knots, set there so thickly
it must have taken years for ladies to stitch them
back in their chambers.
The crown was worth more
that encircled his head –
made of diamonds
both bright and crystal clear.

Then they brought him his shield of heraldic red
with the pentangle engraved in bright gold colours. 620
He took it by the strap and pulled it round his neck,
and it fitted him wonderfully well.
And why the pentangle was so apt for this knight
I'm now going to tell you, even if it's digressing.
What it is is a symbol that Solomon devised
to represent truth in balance with justice,

because it is a figure with five points,
each line overlapping and interlocking with the rest
so it has no end. It is called, I believe,
630 'the endless knot', in all parts of England.
It's attached to this knight and his flawless arms,
because Gawain was reputed in five ways faithful,
and five times over; refined as pure gold,
devoid of all sin and marked with virtue
wherever he went.
That's why he displayed
this pentangle on his shield,
as the man of truest fame
and most pure in his speech.

640 First he was faultless in all his five senses;
next, he never failed in his five fingers,
and all his trust was in the five wounds
of Christ on the cross, as the Bible describes.
And whenever this knight was hard pressed in battle,
his firm belief, above all else,
was that his strength came from the five joys
that the noble queen of heaven took in her child.
It was fitting then that Gawain had
her image depicted inside his shield,
650 so when he looked at it his heart would not falter.
The fifth five virtues that Gawain maintained
were generosity and sympathy first of all,
chastity and courtesy which he never failed in,
and above all compassion. These five things
were fixed more firmly in him than anyone else.
And all five were rooted in this knight,
each locked to the next so that there was no end
or beginning to any: fixed and unwavering,
neither overlaying nor divided on any side,
660 without end at a corner to be found anywhere,
no matter at which point you started to test them.
On his shield this device was marked out
with red gold on a red background.

'The pure pentangle', the people called it
traditionally.
Now fine Gawain is ready,
he takes his lance at once
and bids them all farewell –
as he thought, for evermore.

He spurred on his horse which sprang on its way, 670
with a force that made fire spark off the stones.
All who watched him sighed in their hearts,
and all of them said the same to one another,
concerned for their hero: 'By Christ, it's a pity
that you will be lost, unrivalled as you are.
It would be hard to find your equal in this world.
It would have been better to act with more caution
so that this brave man ended up as a duke.
He seems likely to have proved a brilliant leader,
which would have been better than certain
destruction, 680
beheaded by some ogre out of foolish pride.
Who ever knew a king to agree to such action
over some silly competition such as knights have at
Christmas?'
Many a tear flowed from their eyes
when the handsome knight set off from the court
that day.
He did not delay
but set out on his quest.
Many a wild road he went
as the book reports. 690

While this hero rode through the whole of England,
Sir Gawain in God's cause, it seemed far from a game.
Often, friendless, he spent the night on his own,
seeing before him nothing to please him.
Through woods and valleys his sole comrade was his
horse,
as he had no one to speak to except for his Maker,

till he'd travelled nearly as far as North Wales.
The islands round Anglesey he held to his left,
crossing the fords along the high headlands
700 by the Holy Head, till he returned to the shore
by the wilds of the Wirral, where very few live
loved either by God or by men of goodwill.
Continually he enquired of everyone he met
if they knew anything about a green knight
or a green chapel anywhere round there.
And they all said no, that never in their lives
had they seen a person of such a colour
as green.
The knight took strange routes
710 over many joyless hills.
His spirits would falter often
before he'd see the chapel.

He struggled up cliffs in godforsaken regions,
as, far from his friends, he wandered as a stranger.
At every ford and stream that the warrior passed,
it was rare if he found no foe to face him,
so savage and aggressive that he had to fight it.
He faced so many trials there in the hills
I couldn't recount a small fraction of them.
720 At times he fought dragons, sometimes wolves,
or trolls of the forest that skulked in the crags.
He fought wild bulls and bears and boars as well,
and giants who stalked him from the fells above.
If he hadn't been alert, and helped by the Lord,
he would certainly often have gone to his death.
But, bad as the fighting was, the winter was worse,
as the ice-cold water poured from the clouds
and froze before it hit the grey ground.
Nearly killed by the sleet, he slept in his armour
730 night after night in naked rocks,
where cold streams clattered down from the heights
or hung over his head in hard spears of ice.

Thus in danger and pain and terrible weather
the knight rode through the wilds, all alone
until Christmas.
Devoutly at that season
he appealed to Our Lady,
to tell him where to ride
to find some resting place.

One morning he rode in good heart by a hillside 740
into a deep forest, endlessly wide,
high hills on both sides and below him dense woods
of huge ancient oaks, massed in their hundreds.
Hazel and hawthorn were tangled together,
covered all over by rough, ragged moss,
with desolate birds on the bare branches,
all piping pitifully from the pain of the cold.
The man on Gryngolet passed beneath them
through swamps and through boglands, all on his
own,
concerned for his obligations in case he should fail 750
to honour the Lord who, that very night,
was born of a maiden to soften our sorrows.
And so, sighing, he said, 'I beg you, Lord,
and Mary the dearest and mildest of mothers,
for some shelter where I may devoutly hear Mass
and Matins tomorrow. Most humbly I ask
and say my "Our Father", "Hail Mary"
and Creed.'
He prayed as he rode
and wept for all his sins. 760
Many times he blessed himself,
saying 'Christ's Cross be my help!'

He had hardly blessed himself three times
before he saw, in the wood, a moated dwelling
on a mound above the plain, closed in by the branches
of huge tree trunks all round its ramparts:

the finest castle a knight ever owned,
pitched on a meadow with a park all around it
and a spiked palisade, densely constructed,
770 surrounded by trees for two miles and more.
From the outside he stared at the keep
as it shimmered and shone through mighty oaks.
Then he took off his helmet and fervently thanked
Christ and Saint Julian who had both shown him favour,
safely leading him and hearing his prayer.
'Now I pray,' he said, 'for good hospitality.'
Then he spurred on Gryngolet with his gold heels
and came by good fortune to the main gate
that led him directly to the end of the drawbridge
780 straight ahead.
The bridge was fully raised,
the gates firmly shut,
the walls, well protected,
secure from winter's blast.

The man sat on his horse, which stopped at the edge
of the deep double ditch that led to the castle.
The walls went a great depth down in the water
and then towered aloft to a huge height,
up to the cornices and the top buttresses,
790 made of massive stone perfectly masoned.
Elegant watchtowers rose up symmetrically
with well-crafted casements that closed to perfection.
A finer castle he had never set eyes on.
Inside he could see a soaring hall,
with ornamental turrets the full length of it
and matching round towers. It was amazingly long,
all topped with capstones artfully carved.
He gazed on the many chalk-white chimneys
that shone blindingly on the roofs of the towers.
800 So many bleach-white pinnacles soaring there,
clustered so thickly on the castle's battlements
that it looked as if it was cut out of paper.

From outside on horseback Gawain thought it
glorious.
If only he could get inside those walls
and shelter in that castle for the holy season
in comfort!
He called, and there soon appeared
a watchman overhead,
who courteously asked
what the wandering knight desired. 810

'Good Sir,' said Gawain, 'would you please bear my
message
to the lord of this castle, my appeal for shelter.'
'By Saint Peter, I will,' said the porter, 'and I am sure
you will be welcome to stay here as long as you like.'
He went away quickly and soon he was back
with a fine company, who welcomed Gawain.
They let down the drawbridge, poured out in
welcome
and fell to their knees on the freezing earth
to greet this guest in the way they thought fit.
They motioned him to the gate, drawn wide as
it was. 820
He asked them to stand and rode over the bridge.
Several held his saddle while he alighted
and a group of them stabled his horse.
Knights and squires came thronging down
to lead him with ceremony into the hall.
When he lifted his helmet, they all rushed forward
to help this guest by taking it from his hands,
and to take too his sword and his shield.
Then he warmly greeted each of those courtiers,
and many proud men competed to honour him. 830
They clothed him richly and led him to the hall,
where a fine fire blazed in the hearth.
Then the lord of the company came from his chamber
to greet him in the hall with every due honour.

He said, 'You are welcome to use as you wish
everything here. All is yours to have and to hold
to your heart's content.'
'Thank you,' said Gawain,
'and may Christ repay you for it.'
840 As men of similar manners
they embraced each other.

Gawain gazed at this man who'd received him so
kindly
and admired this fine figure who governed the castle,
a powerful man in the prime of life.
His red beard was broad and luxuriant;
he was vigorously built with muscular legs.
His face was fire-red, and his speech was polite.
He seemed well suited, so Gawain thought,
to lead a hall company of cultivated lords.
The master showed him his room, and gave clear
850 orders
to bring a servant who would graciously attend to him.
There were plenty of volunteers to answer his bidding
and lead him to a chamber with handsome bed-drapes.
The silk curtains were hemmed with bright gold
and the counterpanes artfully panelled,
with white fur at the top and embroidered sides.
The curtains were strung on gold-red rings;
silk textiles from Tars and Toulouse hung on the
walls,
and the same on the floor under his feet.
860 With admiring words the man was relieved
of his coat of mail and his splendid clothes.
Then quickly they brought him handsome robes,
to choose which he liked best and have it put on.
As soon as he chose one he'd like to be dressed in,
it looked fine on him with its flowing skirts.
He seemed in appearance to everyone there
like a vision of spring, with all his limbs covered
in the most glowing and brilliant colours.

Christ never created a handsomer knight,
they all thought. 870
From wherever he came,
it seemed as if he must
be a prince without equal
in the field where fierce men fought.

Before the fireplace, where charcoal burned,
a chair fit for Gawain was duly placed,
with quilted cushions, delicately worked.
A coloured cloak of shining silk
was spread on his shoulders, embroidered ornately
and lined inside with the finest furs, 880
all genuine ermine – his hood was the same.
He sat on his very luxurious seat
and warmed himself through till his spirits rose.
Soon a table was set up neatly on trestles,
covered with a bright cloth of brilliant white,
then a tablecloth, salvers and silver spoons.
He washed in comfort and went to his food.
With the greatest civility the servants brought
various stews, most richly seasoned,
in double portions. There were all kinds of fish: 890
some baked in bread, some roasted on coals,
some boiled, some stewed and flavoured with spices,
and all with subtle sauces to tempt the knight's
palate.
He called it a banquet, again and again,
when they graciously begged him,
'Please for now
take this penitential fare.
Later it will be better.'
The man was full of merriment:
the wine had gone to his head. 900

Then the prince was questioned, with all due tact,
through polite requests that they put to him,
till he modestly admitted what court he came from,

where Arthur the valiant and noble held sway
as powerful lord of the royal Round Table,
and that it was indeed Gawain who sat there,
arrived that Christmas as chance had arranged it.
When the lord discovered that he had that knight
he laughed out loud, he was so overjoyed,
910 and all in the court took the greatest delight
in appearing quickly in the presence of Gawain,
to whose name was attached all glory and fame
for refinement of virtue, and who was everywhere
praised.
Of all men in the world his honour is greatest.
Everyone quietly said to his neighbour,
'Now will we see refinement in practice
and the flawless terms of proper speech.
We will learn how to excel in unlaboured speaking,
since we have here the master of manners.
920 God has indeed given us His grace in plenty,
in granting us to have such a guest as Gawain,
at the season when people gather to rejoice at His birth
and sing.
In the art of pure manners
this man will now instruct us.
I believe whoever listens
will learn all about love-talking.'

By the time dinner was over and the prince had stood
up,
it had nearly come to the fall of night.
930 The chaplains made their way to the chapel
and rang the bells loudly, as they had to
for the high evensong of that great feast day.
The lord responded and the lady also;
she gracefully entered a beautiful pew,
and Gawain happily made his way there as well.
The lord took his sleeve and led him to his seat,
greeted him by name in the friendliest way,
and declared him the most welcome person alive.

Gawain thanked him heartily, and after embracing,
they sat together quietly throughout the service. 940
The lady wanted a look at the knight
as she came from her pew with all her fine ladies.
She was the most beautiful, both in body and face,
of figure and manners, of all of them there;
more beautiful than Guinevere, Gawain reflected,
as she came through the chapel to greet her guest.
Another woman led her by the left hand,
older than she was – a venerable lady,
much reverenced by those noble people.
These ladies were very unalike in appearance, 950
for the younger was fresh, while the other was
withered.
Bright red adorned the first lady all over;
rough wrinkled cheeks hung slack on the other.
The young one wore scarves and many bright pearls;
her breast and white throat exposed to view
shone brighter than new-fallen snow on the hillside.
The old lady's neck was covered by a wimple,
pulled over her sallow chin with chalk-white veils.
Her forehead was masked in silk, muffled all over,
covered and screened with jewellery all round, 960
so nothing could be seen but her grey eyebrows,
her eyes and nose and her bare lips,
which were ghastly to look at and horribly chapped.
Hardly to be thought a worldly beauty,
the Lord save us!
Her body was short and fat,
her buttocks spreading wide.
Nicer to look upon
was her companion for sure!

When Gawain saw that beauty who gazed on him
sweetly, 970
with the lord's approval he stepped out to meet them.
He embraced the old lady, bowing down low,
and, taking the other lightly in his arms,

kissed her with grace and spoke with charm.
They asked for his friendship, and he quickly begged
to be their true servant, if it wouldn't displease them.
Then they took him between them, in keen
conversation,
led him to the fireplace and called out at once
for dessert, which men hastened to bring in
abundance,
980 with extravagant wines for every dish.
The lord very often sprang to his feet,
asking for happiness to be on all sides.
He swept off his hood, which he hung on a spear
and dared them to win the honour to hold it
so the greatest delight might last throughout Christmas.
'And I will try, I promise, to vie with the best
in protecting this garment with the help of my friends.'
So with laughing words the lord leads the way
to amuse Sir Gawain and the retainers in hall
990 that night,
until the time had come
to call for the night lights.
Sir Gawain took his leave
and set off for his bed.

Next morning, when all people observe the time
that Our Lord was born to die for our good,
there is joy for His sake in each earthly dwelling.
It was the same in the castle with comforts of all kinds;
at every mealtime accomplished chefs
1000 prepared subtle dishes to grace the high table.
The elderly lady sat in the top place,
and the lord, I imagine, sat chivalrously by her.
Gawain and the fair lady were sitting together,
just in the middle where the servers came first,
before passing in turn to the rest of the hall.
Once all had been served according to rank,
there was food and delight and general rejoicing,

which wouldn't be easy for me to describe
even supposing I had the patience to try.
But this much I know: Gawain and the lady 1010
took so much pleasure in each other's company
through the sweet endearments of their elegant words,
with proper speech, free of dishonour,
that their play surpassed any pastime of princes
no doubt about it.
Trumpets and kettledrums
and pipes rang out,
with each man set on pleasure,
as those two were on theirs.

Much joy was made there that day and the next, 1020
and the following day too was spent in delight.
The celebration for Saint John's Day was marvellous to hear
and marked the end of feasting, as people there thought.
Since the guests had to leave in the grey of dawn,
they stayed up very late, drinking the wine,
and danced without pausing the finest set pieces.
Finally, very late, they all took their leave,
each visitor going on his way.
As Gawain bade goodnight, the noble lord detained him
and brought him to his own room, close to the chimney. 1030
There he held him back, warmly thanking him
for the joyful honour that he had conferred
by visiting his castle in that festive season
and enriching the household with his graceful presence.
'As long as I live, Sir, I will be the better
for the visit of Gawain at God's highest feast.'
'Thank you,' said Gawain, 'but in truth all the honour
is yours – may the High King of heaven reward you.
And I am your servant, to act out your will

1040 as now I'm obliged to on every occasion
as of right.'
The lord did all he could
to make the knight stay on.
But Gawain assured him
that he could not do that.

Then the lord asked him directly
what pressing cause in that holiday season
made him determined to ride alone from the court,
before the feast days were wholly over.
1050 'Indeed, Sir,' the knight said, 'that's a good question.
An urgent mission drove me from my court,
because I am committed to seek out a place,
and I don't know where in the world to search.
For all the land in England I wouldn't want to fail
to find it by New Year's morning, so help me God!
So, Sir, now I appeal to you
to tell me if by any chance you know
of the Green Chapel, or on what ground it stands,
and of the knight who lives there, whose colour is
green.
1060 Between the two of us we made an agreement
that I would meet him there if I lived,
and we're a short time away from our New Year
deadline.
If God gave me such a favour, I'd see that knight
more happily, by God's son, than possess any riches.
So, with your permission, I must certainly go,
for I now have left but a bare three days,
and I'd rather fall dead than fail in this task.'
Then, laughing, the lord said, 'Well, now you can stay.
I can direct you there in plenty of time.
No longer fret about the Green Chapel's
1070 whereabouts.
You will stay in your comfortable bed
till late in the morning, then set off at New Year,

and be there by mid-morning to do what you want
in that spot.
Stay until New Year's Day;
get up and set off then.
Someone will lead the way.
It's less than two miles off.'

Then Gawain was happy and laughed with good
cheer.
'I thank you most for this, beyond everything else. 1080
Now my success is assured, at your request
I will stay on and do whatever you say.'
Then the lord clasped him and sat by his side,
bidding the ladies be brought to cheer them still
further
and they all sat together with the greatest enjoyment.
The lord in good humour said such cheerful things,
like a man losing his reason, who didn't know what to
do next.
Then he called to the knight, shouting out loud:
'You've undertaken to do what I ask;
will you keep that promise, at this very moment?' 1090
'Most certainly, yes,' Gawain replied.
'While I stay in your house, I am bound to your will.'
'You have come far,' said the lord, 'made a long
journey
and sat late with me, so you're not well recovered
in food or in sleep, I am certain of that.
You must stay late in your room, lie at your ease
until Mass-time tomorrow, and go to your meals
whenever you want, with my wife who'll stay with you
and cheer you with her company until I get home.
You stay here; 1100
I'll get up early
and go out to the hunt.'
Gawain happily
agreed to his wish.

'One more thing,' said the lord, 'let's make an
agreement.
What I gain in the woods will be given to you
in exchange for whatever your luck gives you here.
Dear friend, let us swear to make such a swap,
whether we fare better or worse.'
1110 'All right,' said Gawain, 'I am happy with that,
and it suits me, if you want, to play such a game.'
'Let a drink be brought to secure the agreement,'
said the lord of the castle, and both of them laughed.
They drank and lingered and acted light-heartedly,
these lords and ladies, for as long as it pleased them.
And then with French manners and elegant speeches,
they stood and conversed and quietly spoke,
before courteously kissing and taking their leave.
Each of them was finally brought to their bed
1120 by willing servants with blazing torches,
privately.
But before they went to bed
they repeated their agreement.
The expert lord and ruler
knew how to run a game.

III

Long before daybreak the people were up.
Guests who had to leave summoned their servants,
and they busily set about saddling the horses,
tackling them up and packing their bags.
They dressed themselves in riding habits, 1130
mounted quickly and took hold of the reins,
each setting off wherever he wanted.
The good lord of the palace was by no means the last
getting ready to ride, with his many attendants.
He ate a quick bite after he had heard Mass
and set off with his horn to the open fields.
By the time the first light had dawned on the earth
he and his men were mounted on horseback.
Then the skilful huntsmen leashed their hounds,
opened the kennels and called them out, 1140
with three loud, ringing notes on their bugles.
The hounds bayed in answer and made a
commotion.
Those that ran off were whipped back and checked
by a hundred hunters of the very best,
so the story says.
The dogmen took their stations
and the huntsmen slipped the leash.
To their loud blasts
the whole forest rang.

At the first sound of the hunt the wild creatures
1150 panicked.
Deer plunged through the valleys, crazy with fear.
They raced to the heights but were quickly forced back
by the circle of beaters with their deafening shouts.
They let the stags go, with their towering heads,
their muscular backs and their high antlers,
for the lord had strictly forbidden disturbance
of the deer in the close season.
The hinds were rounded up with 'How!' and 'Hup!',
and the does driven in uproar to the lower ground.
1160 You could watch as they rained their slanting arrows.
At each point of the wood a shower of them flew,
and their broad heads brutally bit into brown flesh.
They screamed and they bled and they died on the
hills,
and the careering dogs pursued them with frenzy.
Hunters with loud horns chased in pursuit
with ringing calls nearly cracking the cliffs.
Such creatures as escaped the vigilant marksmen
were pulled down and ripped apart at the hides,
once they'd been driven down to the river.
1170 The men were skilled at those lower stations,
and their massive greyhounds fell on those beasts
quickly
and hauled them to ground straightaway
in the blink of an eye.
The lord, delirious with delight,
rode, dismounted again,
and spent the day in excitement
right to the fall of night.

While the lord was busy by the borders of the wood
the bold Gawain kept to his soft bed.
1180 He lay there till daylight shone on the walls,
beneath his bright bedspread, screened all around.
As he dozed there in peace, he warily heard
a little noise at the door as it stealthily opened.

He raised his head up out of the clothes
and slightly lifted the edge of the curtain,
peeping out cautiously to see what it was.
It was the lady, most lovely to look at,
who shut the door after her, in secret and privately,
and stole towards the bed. The hero, embarrassed,
lay hurriedly back down, pretending to sleep. 1190
She stepped forward silently and stole to his bedside,
lifted the curtain and crept inside,
sitting down softly on the edge of the bed.
And there she stayed, to see if he'd wake up.
The hero lay low some considerable time,
pondering inwardly what all this might mean
or amount to. It seemed pretty strange,
but still he said to himself, 'It would be more fitting
to ask her openly what she is after.'
So he awoke and stretched and, turning
towards her, 1200
opened his eyes, pretending to be surprised.
Then, as if to be safer by prayer, he blessed himself
with his hand.
With her pretty chin, and cheeks
of mingled red and white,
she spoke most sweetly
with her small, laughing lips.

'Good morning, Sir Gawain,' said the lovely lady,
'you're a careless sleeper, to let someone creep
up on you like this. You're caught. Unless there's a
truce, 1210
I'll besiege you in bed, you can be sure.'
Laughing away she made jokes like that.
'Good morning, fair lady,' said Gawain, all good
humour.
'I am at your service, and delighted to be so;
I surrender at once and sue for mercy:
the best policy since I have no option.'
And so he joked in return, with cheerful laughter.

'But if, lovely lady, you'd grant me this –
to release your prisoner, and ask him to stand,
1220 I'd get out of this bed and dress myself better;
I would talk to you then in the greatest comfort.'
'No indeed, handsome Sir,' the fair lady said,
'you are not getting up. I've a better plan for you.
I'll besiege you on the other flank too,
and then negotiate with my knight that I've caught;
because I know well that you are Sir Gawain
that the whole world worships wherever you go.
Your honour and accomplishment are highly praised
by lords and by ladies and by everyone living.
1230 And here you are now, and just us two.
My husband and his men are gone far afield;
everyone else is in bed; my ladies are too.
The door is shut, securely locked.
Since I have in my house everyone's favourite,
I will spend my time well, as long as it lasts,
in talk.
You are welcome to my body
to exercise your power.
I am obliged, and willing,
1240 to bend to your greater strength.'

'Well,' said Gawain, 'this is a privilege,
but I am far from what you describe.
I am unworthy to rise to such honour
as you suggest here; I know myself well.
If such was your wish, by God I'd be pleased
if I might be of service in word or in deed
to serve your goodwill – it would be pure joy.'
'Now truly, Sir Gawain,' said the beautiful lady,
'if I should undervalue the prowess and standing
1250 that please everyone else, it would be no credit.
There are plenty of women who would much rather have
you, noble Sir, as I have you here,
interchanging fine words with you,

to bring them comfort and soothe their cares,
than most of the treasure or goods that they have.
But I praise the Lord that rules the high heavens
that I've here in my hands what everyone wants
by the sheerest good fortune.'
She, of such beauty,
was so flattering to him, 1260
and the knight with proper speech
replied to all she said.

'Madame,' said Gawain, 'may Our Lady reward you,
for your kindness to me is generous indeed.
But people often form judgements on rumour,
and I do not deserve the acclaim that they give.
It is to your credit that you think only goodness.'
'By Mary,' the lady said, 'I don't believe that;
for if I were as worthy as any woman living,
and all the wealth of the world were at my disposal, 1270
and I bargained for ever to find a good partner,
from your behaviour that I have seen here –
your good looks and grace and kindly demeanour,
which I'd heard of before and now find to be true –
no man on earth would be chosen before you.'
'Noble lady,' he said, 'you're certainly matched better.
But still I am honoured by your good opinion
and, as your humble servant, I hold you my ruler
and declare myself your knight. May Christ reward
you!'
So they talked on till past the mid-morning, 1280
with the lady acting as if she loved him.
The knight held his ground and behaved very well,
considering her beauty and what she'd in mind.
There was less love in him because of the hardship
he'd shortly to face,
the blow that will strike him,
as it must come about.
So when she spoke of leaving,
he readily agreed.

Then she bade him good day and glanced at him,
1290 laughing.
But as she stood up, her fierce words appalled him.
'May whoever rewards talking repay you for this;
but that you are Gawain can not be believed.'
'Why?' said the knight in eager enquiry,
afraid he'd come short in some detail of manners.
The lady blessed him and said, 'For this reason:
someone who is reputed as accomplished as Gawain,
with manners developed so perfectly in him,
could hardly have sat so long with a lady
1300 without begging a kiss in the name of courtesy,
by some hint or other at the end of conversing.'
Then Gawain said, 'Please, let us do what you wish:
I will kiss at your command, as a knight's duty is,
and do more rather than offend you, so don't ask
again.'
She came near and took him within her arms,
bending down sweetly, and kissed her hero.
They commended each other duly to Christ,
and she went out the door with no further dispute.
He hurried to get up, urgently calling
1310 his chamberlain and choosing his clothes.
As soon as he was ready he set off happily
to Mass, and then to his food which was waiting.
Then he relaxed the whole day with great pleasure,
until the moon rose.
Never was man placed better
between such worthy ladies,
the older and the young.
Such joy they had together!

All this time, the lord was at his sport,
1320 hunting barren hinds in heathland and wood.
He'd slain so many by the time the sun set,
does and other creatures, it's hard to describe.
Then at last the hunters came flocking back in
and quickly made a pile of the slaughtered deer.

The leaders arrived there with troops of their
followers,
selected the animals with the most flesh on them,
and cut them open by the most skilful means.
Some of them first examined the brisket
and found a good two fingers of flesh in the leanest.
They cut through the throat, seized hold of the
gullet, 1330
cut it with a sharp blade and tied up the gut.
They cut off the four legs and stripped the hides,
opened the belly and pulled out the bowels,
careful not to break the knot on the gut.
They grasped the throat and rapidly severed
the gullet from the windpipe, and pulled out the
entrails.
They cut out the shoulders with their sharp butchers'
knives,
pulling them through a small gap to keep the hide
whole.
They cut open the breast and pulled it in two.
Next they returned again to the gullet, 1340
slitting it quickly right back to the hind-fork.
They pulled out the guts, and then after that
swiftly cut the membranes clean off the ribs.
They skilfully worked along the backbone,
trimmed it off to the haunch so it hung in one piece,
and lifted it up whole to cut it off there.
That's what they call the numbles I think,
strictly speaking.
By the fork of the thighs
they cut the skin behind. 1350
Next they sever them,
dividing down the ridge.

Then they cut off the head and the neck,
and they sundered the sides at once from the spine.
They flung the raven's portion into the branches.
They pierced through the tough skin at the ribs

and hung it up at both sides by the four hocks.
Then each man received his personal share.
They fed their hounds on the handsome beast's skin,
1360 with the liver and lights, the skin of the stomach
and blood-soaked bread mixed in with it all.
Loudly they blew the kill to the baying of the hounds.
Then they took up their meat and set off for home,
loudly blaring out their echoing call.
By the time daylight was gone the company had
reached
the glorious castle where the knight waited,
lying low,
happy by the blazing fire.
The lord came in,
1370 and when Gawain met him
it was all friendly goodwill.

The lord bade the household to gather in the hall,
and asked both the ladies to come down with their
maidens
before the assembly. He told the servants
to bring all the venison in there before them,
and eagerly called Gawain, in the height of good
humour,
pointing to the tails still whole on the beasts
and the clean flesh sheared from the ribs.
'Does this sport impress you? Have I merited praise?
1380 Have I not earned rich reward by my skills?'
'Yes indeed,' replied Gawain, 'this is the best haul
I have seen in the season this past seven years.'
'And I give it all to you, Gawain,' said the lord.
'By the compact we made you can call it your own.'
'That is true,' said Gawain. 'And I confirm too,
that what I've won fairly here in the castle
with equal good grace will be given to you.'
He clasped his fine neck with both of his arms
and kissed him as gracefully as he knew how.
1390 'You take my winnings. That is all I gained here.

I'd yield it up freely, even if it were more.'
'It's fine,' said the nobleman. 'Thank you for that.
It might even be better if you were to tell me
where you won this fine prize by your own single
efforts.'
'That wasn't our agreement,' said he. 'Ask me no more.
You've taken what was owing and you must not expect
anything further.'
They laughed and passed the time
with pleasurable talk.
Then they went to supper 1400
and yet more fine fare.

Afterwards they sat in the room by the chimney,
where servants brought in the best wine without pause,
and in the end they agreed that again the next morning
they'd give an undertaking the same as before:
that whatever might happen, they'd exchange their
winnings,
the new things they'd won when they met again at
night.
They made firm that agreement before the whole
court,
and more drink was brought with the highest good
humour.
Affectionately they parted at the end of the evening, 1410
and each of them went straight to their bed.
By the time that the cock had clarioned three times,
the lord had leaped from bed, and all of his followers.
Once the food and the Mass were duly observed,
the party hastened to the woods, before day dawned,
back on the hunt.
With the hunters and the horns
they careered over the plains.
Unleashed among the briars,
the hounds ran on ahead. 1420

Soon they bayed for a scenting, down by the marsh
side.
The hunters urged on the hounds that first found it,
shouting out wildly in the greatest excitement.
The pack heard them and bounded there quickly.
They fell at once on the spoor, forty together,
and such a commotion and racket of hounds
arose that the rocky banks rang all around.
Hunters encouraged them with horn-blowing and
shouting.
Then all in a pack they surged on together,
1430 between a pool in the forest and a lowering crag.
In a corner by a cliff, to the side of the marsh,
where the rugged rock had treacherously crumbled,
they came on their prey, with the men on their tails.
The hunt ringed the crag and the thicket beside it,
until they knew well what was lurking inside,
what beast it was that the bloodhounds had scented.
Then they beat on the bushes to make it break cover,
and it madly plunged out through the lines of men:
the most amazing wild boar dashed out in full view,
1440 long out of the herd because of his age.
He was powerful indeed, the biggest conceivable,
and he roared ferociously. Some of them felt it,
for at the first thrust he threw three to the ground
and dashed off at full speed without further damage.
The others yelled loudly, crying out 'Hoi!',
horns to their mouths to summon the dogs.
The men and the hounds raised tumultuous uproar,
dashing after this boar, with outcry and bedlam,
up for the kill.
1450 Often he turned at bay
and maimed the pack as he fought.
He injured many hounds,
who yelped pitifully.

Next on the scene were men to shoot at him,
loosing their arrows and hitting him repeatedly.

But the points were blunted, striking his shoulders,
and the barbs were unable to pierce through his brow.
The shaven shafts shattered in pieces,
and the arrowheads bounced back wherever they
struck.
But when the blows of their missiles caused him
pain, 1460
brain-mad from baiting, he rushed on the men,
injuring them grievously as he charged out upon them,
so that many shrank away and drew themselves back.
The lord on his lively horse took up the pursuit,
like a brave man in battle blowing his bugle.
He sounded the recall and rode through thick bushes,
pursuing this wild boar till the sun's beams had set.
They spent the whole day with this kind of hunting,
while our lovely Gawain lay in his bed,
in his elegant chamber in opulent clothes 1470
of bright colours.
The lady did not forget
to come to him in greeting.
She was with him good and early
to try and change his heart.

She came to the curtain and peeped at the knight.
Sir Gawain welcomed her politely at once,
and she readily repaid him with her kind words.
She sat down by him softly, freely laughed with him,
and with a look full of love she tried these words: 1480
'Sir, it seems to me a wonder if you really are Gawain,
a man so unfailingly of the greatest propriety,
that you're not better versed in society's manners.
And even when taught them, they go from your mind.
You've already forgotten what I taught you yesterday
with the clearest lesson I am capable of.'
'What is that?' said the knight. 'I really don't know;
if what you say is true, I am greatly at fault.'
'But I taught you to kiss,' said the beautiful lady.
'When the willingness is there, claim it at once. 1490

That's the rule for the knight who practises courtliness.'
'Dear lady,' said the brave man, 'do not say that.
I dared not do it lest I might be refused.
If I were refused, it would be wrong to have offered.'
'But in fact,' said the lady, 'you can't be refused;
you're strong enough to win by force if you want,
if anyone were ill-bred enough to refuse you.'
'Yes indeed,' said Gawain. 'That's true of course.
But threats are not right in the country I come from,
1500 nor any gift valued that is not made freely.
I am at your bidding, to kiss when you like.
Take when you want, and leave when you want,
here and now.'
The lady bent down
to sweetly kiss his face.
And much they conversed
of the pains and joy of love.

'I'd like you to tell me,' said the worthy lady,
'if it did not offend you, what the fashion is now
1510 with someone as young and fit as you are,
so courteous, so chivalric as you're known to be –
since of all parts of chivalry the most to be praised
is the true pursuit of love, the bible of knightliness.
For, speaking of the play of principled knights,
this is the proof and core of their deeds:
how men for true love have risked their lives,
endured for their passion terrible times,
taking action to cure their pain by their courage,
bringing bliss to the chamber with their singular feats.
1520 You are known as the very best knight of your time;
talk and praise of you are heard everywhere.
I have sat by you here on two occasions
without hearing from your lips a single word
bearing on love, high up or low down.
You, so courteous and mannerly with vows,
ought to be willing to teach a young person
and show her some details of true love's skills.

So, are you ignorant, despite this repute?
Or do you think me too stupid to grasp your finesse?
It's a shame. 1530
I've come here alone, and sit
hoping to learn some skill.
Come on, teach me something
while my husband's far from home.'

'May God reward you!' said Gawain, 'I swear
it's the greatest privilege and delight for me
that someone as gifted as you would come
and bother to play with so poor a knight
in any spirit: it gives me great joy.
But to take on the task of pronouncing on love, 1540
of preaching the niceties and stories of feats
to you who, I'm sure, know twice as much
of the wiles of that art than a hundred like me
could ever aspire to in the country I come from,
would be reckless presumption, I am sure, dear lady.
I will meet your request as well as I can
because I'm greatly indebted, and will evermore
be your true servant, as God is my judge.'
So the lady besought him, and repeatedly tried
to urge him towards wooing, whatever her plan
was; 1550
but he parried so well that he seemed without fault,
guiltless on both fronts, and they experienced nothing
but pleasure.
They laughed and played a long time
until finally she kissed him,
said a sweet goodbye
and went away at last.

Gawain bestirred himself and got ready for Mass,
and their meal was prepared and formally served.
There with the ladies he enjoyed the whole day, 1560
while the lord, without pausing, rode over the
country

with his gruesome boar that raced through the hills,
biting in two the best hounds' backs
where he stood at bay. The bowmen flushed him out
at last, forced unwillingly into the open
by the arrows that rained down where the hunt was
assembled.
But still he made the bravest men flinch,
till at last he was done and could run no more.
As fast as he could, he got to a hole
1570 in a cliff near a boulder, where a stream ran by.
With his back to the hill he started scraping the
ground,
froth foaming from his ghastly mouth's corners,
and whetted his white tusks. All the valiant men
who stood nearby had had more than enough
of the chase from afar, but they dared not go closer
because of the danger.
He had injured so many
he'd made them all wary
of being torn by his tusks.
1580 He was brave, and maddened too.

Then the lord came himself, urging his steed on,
and saw the boar at bay with the men all around him.
He dismounted swiftly, leaving his horse,
pulled out his bright sword and bravely advanced,
wading through the stream where the fierce beast
stood.
When the boar saw the man with his weapon in hand
his bristles stood up and he snorted ferociously,
so they feared that the worst might befall their lord.
The boar drove out, straight for the knight,
1590 so that they fell in a heap, man and pig,
where the water ran fastest. But the boar came off
worse,
for the knight eyed him well as they came to grips
and plunged his blade firmly, right in his throat,

pierced to the hilt so his heart burst in two
and, snarling, he surrendered, swept down the stream
    at high speed.
  A hundred hounds fell on him
  and savagely started to bite.
  The men dragged him to land
  and the dogs killed him off. 1600

Then was proud blaring on many a horn,
loud yelling by noblemen that still had the breath for it.
Dogs bayed at the beast, set on by their masters,
who'd been the lead-huntsmen in that wearying chase.
Then a man who was expert in the woodsman's art
began with great care to cut up the boar.
First he cut off the head and impaled it high up,
and then split him roughly along the backbone.
He pulled out the bowels to burn on a fire,
mixing them with bread as reward for the dogs. 1610
Then he cut out the flesh in thick white chunks
and pulled out the offal in the recognized sequence.
Last, he tied the two halves back together
and on a strong pole hung them securely.
Now with this beast they set off for home,
with the boar's head carried ahead of the man
that had killed him so valiantly by the might of his hand
    there in the stream.
  He could hardly wait
  until he saw Gawain. 1620
  He called, and the knight came fast
  to receive his winnings.

The lord, with his loud voice and ringing laughter,
called out happily when he saw Gawain.
The good ladies were brought and the company
    summoned.
He showed them the meat and told them the tale
of the wild boar's size, and his ferocious

self-defence as he fled through the wood.
Gawain heard of these deeds with great admiration
1630 and praised the lord's exploits in the warmest terms,
for such a huge beast, the brave man declared,
or such sides of meat he'd not seen before.
Then they touched the huge head, while the great
knight praised it,
expressing his horror in the lord's hearing.
'Gawain,' the lord said, 'this trophy is yours,
by our agreement, as you know already.'
'That's true,' said Gawain, 'and equally true
that I'll give you my catch, I swear in good faith.'
He seized him round the neck, and kissed him
warmly,
1640 and immediately after repeated the gift.
'Now we are paid up,' said the knight, 'here this
evening
by all the agreements we made since I got here
in full.'
The lord said, 'By Saint Giles,
you've gained things of great worth.
You'll soon be very wealthy,
if you go on winning so.'

Then they pulled out the trestles to set up the tables
and put fine cloths on them. Next bright lights
1650 were lit along the walls with wax torches.
The servants laid the tables and served the whole
hall.
Much rejoicing and merriment echoed
round the fire in the hall, and noble songs
of every kind were sung at supper and after it,
Christmas part-songs and newly composed carols,
with all the graceful hilarity that could be imagined,
and our fine knight always sat next to the lady.
She showed such signs of favour towards him
with stealthy looks of interest to please the great hero
1660 that he was disconcerted and inwardly anxious;

but because of his chivalry he could not demur,
but showed her every courtesy, whatever might be
    the ultimate outcome.
  When they had amused themselves
  as they wanted in the hall,
  the lord called him to his chamber
  and they drew to the fireside.

There they drank and talked, and the lord proposed
to make the same bargain for New Year's Eve.
But the knight asked leave to ride off in the morning 1670
since it was close to the date that he must observe.
The lord dissuaded him and asked him to stay,
saying, 'On my word of honour, I promise you
that you'll get to the chapel to meet your demands
at the dawn of New Year in the early morning.
So lie in your bed and take your ease,
while I hunt in the wood, and we'll keep the agreement:
to exchange our winnings when I get back here.
I've tested you twice and found you faithful.
Remember in the morning that "Third is final"! 1680
Let's relax while we can and enjoy ourselves here,
for causes of regret are too easily found.'
This was readily agreed, that Gawain would stay.
Quickly drink was brought. Then they went to bed
    by candlelight.
  Sir Gawain lay and slept
  sound and soft all night;
  the lord, with his own plans,
  was up at the first light.

He and his men had some food after Mass. 1690
It was a fine morning and he called for his mount;
all those engaged to ride along with him
were mounted already before the hall gates.
The earth looked a picture: the frost was like steel,
and the risen sun shone red on the mist
as it brightly crossed the clouds of the heavens.

The hunters unleashed by the forest side,
and the rocks in the wood rang to their horn-calls.
Some came on the path where a fox was skulking,
1700 often cross-tracking with his instinctive wiles.
A harrier picked the scent up and the hunters called;
his comrades fell in, panting loudly,
running on in a pack, right on his tail.
The fox ran ahead, but they soon tracked him down.
And, when they caught sight of him, followed him fast,
denouncing him loudly with a terrible racket.
He dodged and doubled through tangles of undergrowth,
turned and listened by the hedges at intervals.
In the end he jumped over a hedge by a ditch,
1710 sneaked out on the quiet by a small wood's edge,
thinking he'd escaped the hounds by his tricks.
But before he could know it, he was in a smart trap,
where three fierce dogs, greyhounds, flung themselves
on him.
He quickly swerved again,
sprang on a new tack,
and in total panic
made off to the wood.

It was sheer joy to hear the hounds then,
1720 when the whole of the meet pursued him at once.
Such an alarm they brought down on his head,
as if the towering cliffs could tumble in fragments.
He was yelled at there when the men came across him,
loudly summoned with a chorus of snarls.
He was threatened and constantly called 'thief',
with harriers on his heels so he couldn't delay.
Always chased down when he attempted a break,
he often dodged back, so wily was Reynard.
He led them in a file, the lord and his company,
1730 all through the hills until mid-afternoon,
while at home the brave knight slept in contentment
inside the fine curtains throughout the cold morning.
But love would not let the lady stay sleeping,

or quell the impulse that stirred in her heart.
She rose up early and made her way
in a stylish dressing-gown that reached to the ground,
elegantly trimmed with refined leather.
No scarf veiled her head, but rich jewels
were set round her coronet in clusters of twenty.
Her lovely face and her neck were exposed, 1740
her upper body bare at the front and the back.
She came inside the bedchamber and closed the door,
pulled open a window and called to the knight,
urgently chivvying him with fine words
and high good humour.
'Come on, man, how can you sleep
this lovely morning?'
He was deep in slumber,
but still he heard her.

In heavy troubled sleep, the knight muttered in
dreams, 1750
like a man who was suffering the deepest anxiety
about what fate destiny would deal him
at the Green Chapel, when he'd meet the knight
and must take his blow without resistance.
But when the woman came in he recovered his thoughts,
escaping his nightmare, and answered at once.
The lovely lady came laughing sweetly,
fell on his handsome face and kissed him with grace.
He welcomed her warmly with proper good manners.
Seeing her so beautiful, so alluringly dressed, 1760
with such perfect features and such a complexion,
his heart swelled with surging joy.
With courteous smiles they turned to their games,
so all was bliss and delight between them,
and pleasure.
They exchanged good words
with much charm in them.
They were in great danger
if Mary had not watched her knight.

1770 For the beautiful lady pressed him so hard,
propositioned him so plainly, that he was obliged
either to take her love or reject her discourteously.
He was worried for his chivalry, in case he'd seem
boorish,
but more for his virtue lest he'd fall into sin
and betray that good lord whose castle it was.
'God forbid,' the knight thought, 'that that should
happen.'
With loving laughter he contrived to deflect
all the words of fondness that fell from her lips.
Said the lady to Gawain, 'You ought to feel shame
1780 not to make love to her you lie next to,
when she is heartsore beyond all lovers on earth,
unless you've a sweetheart, someone you love more
and have sworn to be faithful to, promised so
bindingly
that you cannot break faith. I think that must be it.
So tell me about it, please, I implore you;
by all the love in the world, don't veil the truth
out of deceit.'
The knight said, 'By Saint John,'
and gently he smiled,
1790 'I swear I have no such love
and will not for some time.'

'Well, that,' said the lady, 'is the worst insult of all;
I am answered indeed and that grieves me the most.
Now kiss me in friendship, and I will be gone.
I will grieve through my life, like a girl deep in love.'
She bent with a sigh and kissed him politely.
Then she moved away from him, and said as she stood:
'Just do me the favour, my dear, at our parting,
to give me some token – your glove, for example –
1800 to remind me of you and soften my grief.'
'Indeed,' said Sir Gawain, 'I wish I had on me
my most precious possession to give for your love,
for you've certainly merited many times over

anything I could give in repayment.
But I can't give a love-token of trivial worth:
it would not do you honour to give so little
as a glove for a keepsake from my possessions.
I am here on a quest in unfamiliar terrain
and have no servants to carry treasures in bagfuls.
I regret that, my lady, out of regard for you. 1810
But each man must act in accord with his means,
so don't be offended.'
'No, most noble knight,'
the fairest lady said.
'Though I've nothing of yours,
you must take a gift of mine.'

She offered him a fine ring of the reddest gold
with a proud stone embossed upon it
and flashing beams as bright as the sun.
You can be sure it was worth a fortune. 1820
But the knight refused it and quickly said,
'In God's name, dear lady, I will take no gifts;
I have none to give you so none will I take.'
She offered it again, but he turned down her gift,
and swore firmly that he would not accept it.
She was sorry he said no, but then she added,
'If you refuse my ring as of too high a value
and you do not want to be so much beholden
I will give you my girdle, which will profit you less.'
And quickly she took off the belt from her waist, 1830
tied round the tunic beneath her rich cloak.
It was adorned with green silk and patterned with
gold,
embroidered at the edge by diligent fingers.
She offered it to the knight, and pleadingly begged
that he should accept it, worthless though it was.
He remained adamant that never at all
would he take anything, gold or treasure,
before God gave him grace to achieve his quest there.
'And so I beg you, do not be displeased,

1840 but end your offers, for I'll never agree
to accept them.
I am deeply in your debt
because you are so kind,
and will ever, come what may,
remain your devoted knight.'

'Do you reject this silk,' the lady asked then,
'because it is a slight thing? It seems so, I know.
Look! It *is* little, and it is worth less.
But anyone who knew of a special power it has
1850 might perhaps come to praise it more highly.
For anyone who wears this length of green lace,
as long as he keeps it tied tightly round him,
there's no warrior on earth who is able to hurt him,
and he can't be killed by any means in the world.'
The knight thought about this, and of course it struck
him
how useful it might be for the threat he was facing.
When he got to that chapel to meet his fate,
it would be a fine thing indeed if he could live on.
So he put up with her pleading and allowed her to
speak.
1860 She put the belt round him, pressing him warmly,
and he consented and gave in with good grace.
But she asked him for her sake not to reveal it
but to hide it faithfully away from her husband.
They agreed that no one but the two of themselves
would know of it ever.
He thanked her very warmly
and now in all sincerity.
By the end she'd kissed her knight
for a third time.

1870 Then she departed and left him alone,
for she would get no more joy from Gawain.
When she was gone, he quickly got up,
rose and dressed in the finest clothes

and stowed away the love-lace the lady had given.
He hid it safely, where he'd find it later,
then boldly made his way into the chapel,
where he discreetly implored a priest to teach him
to improve his life and show him better
how to save his soul when it passed from the earth.
Then he confessed clearly and told him his sins, 1880
both great and small, and begged for forgiveness,
asking the priest for complete absolution.
He had penance in full and was shriven as clear
as if the Day of Judgement was fixed for next
morning.
Then he had more pleasure with those fine ladies,
with elegant carols and all kinds of delight,
than ever before that day, until night fell
amid happiness.
Everyone was pleased,
observing that 'certainly 1890
he was never before this happy
since he first arrived here'.

Let him rest there in comfort and may love come to
him!
The lord was still in the fields, leading his men.
He overtook the fox that he'd followed for so long;
he found the villain dashing over a fence,
when he'd heard the hounds who'd pursued him most
fiercely.
Reynard picked his way through a tangled thicket
with the whole pack rushing hard on his trail.
The lord saw the animal and picked his moment. 1900
He drew out his bright sword and struck at the fox,
who ducked from the blade and would have dodged
back,
but a hound leaped upon him, just at that point,
and at the horse's hooves they all fell upon him,
savaging the trickster with fearsome clamour.
The lord dismounted and grabbed him at once,

pulled him smartly from the mouths of the dogs,
held him high over his head, hallooing loudly,
as the fierce hounds bayed all around him.
1910 The hunters hurried there with a flourish of horns,
sounding a long rally till they saw the lord.
By this time the whole hunt had assembled,
with all their bugles blowing together,
and those without horns yelling out themselves.
They raised the liveliest baying that ever was heard,
the loud call that was made for the soul of Reynard
with hue and cry!
They rewarded the gallant hounds,
patting and stroking heads.
1920 Then they took Reynard
and stripped him of his coat.

Then they set off for home, for it was nearly night,
blowing full blast on their ringing horns.
The lord alighted at last at his beloved castle,
where he found a fire in the hall and the knight beside it,
the good Sir Gawain who was pleased about everything,
with the amorous talk he'd had with the ladies.
He wore a blue cloak that stretched to the ground.
His topcoat suited him, trimmed with soft fur,
1930 and his hood of the same hung to his shoulders,
both of them edged with ermine all round.
He met the lord in the middle of the hall
and greeted him cheerfully, graciously saying,
'This time I'll be first fulfilling our bargain,
made for our benefit when the drink wasn't stinted.'
Then he seized the lord and gave him three kisses,
the sweetest and firmest that he could bestow.
'By God,' said the lord, 'you've had much bliss
in gaining this merchandise, if the price was fair.'
1940 'Never mind the price,' Gawain quickly replied,
'since the debt that I owed is openly paid.'
'Well, indeed,' said the other, 'my gift is poorer,
for I have hunted all day and captured nothing

but this wretched fox – the Devil take him! –
and that's poor return for such a trio of things
as you've given me here, three kisses
so delicious.'
'Say no more,' said Gawain.
'I thank you, by the Cross.'
And how the fox was slain 1950
he told him as they stood.

With joy and with music and most appetizing dishes
they celebrated as fully as anyone could,
with the laughter of ladies and elegant talking,
and the lord and Gawain both so delighted,
short of being mad or totally drunk.
Both the lord and his household were full of jokes
till the time came for them to part,
when people at last had to take to their beds.
Modestly the noble knight first took leave 1960
of the great lord, and thanked him with warmth.
'For the wonderful visit that I have made here,
and your honouring me this season, may the High
King reward you!
I pledge myself in exchange for one of your men,
for as you well know I must leave in the morning,
if you can lend, as you offered, a man to direct me
to that Green Chapel, where God will grant
that I take on New Year's Day what fate has in store.'
'In good faith,' said the lord, 'most willingly
everything I promised I'll give you indeed.' 1970
He assigned him a servant to show him the path
and convey him through the hills without losing his way,
to ride through the woods and groves
by the shortest route.
Gawain thanked the lord
for such a courtesy.
Then to those fine ladies
the knight bade farewell.

With regrets and kisses he talked to them both,
1980 and pressed upon them his most fervent thanks.
Quickly they gave him the same in return,
commending him to Christ with sighs of regret.
He left all the company with impeccable manners;
each one he met he thanked individually
for their kindness and service and the pains they had
taken,
how assiduous they had been in serving him well.
Everyone was as sorry to part with him there
as if they'd lived with him the whole of their lives.
He was brought to his room by servants with lights
1990 and happily led to his bed for the night.
Whether he slept well I won't make a guess,
for he had much on his mind with the coming events
in the morning.
But let him lie there still;
he is close to his destiny.
If you keep quiet a while
I'll tell you how things fared.

IV

Now the New Year's approaching, and the night is
passing.
The dawn defeats dark, as the Lord ordains it.
But the worst weather in the world brewed up
outside; 2000
clouds drove the cold down to the ground
with enough of north's sharpness to perish poor
people.
Bitter snow slanted down and stung the wild beasts;
the screaming wind whipped from the heights
and filled every valley with swollen snowdrifts.
The knight listened where he lay in his bed.
Though he closes his eyes, he sleeps very little;
by each crow of the cock he knew well the time.
Quickly he dressed, before the day dawned,
by the glow of the lamps that gleamed in his
chamber. 2010
He called to his servant, who answered at once,
and asked him to bring his armour and saddle.
The man got up and brought him his clothes,
and fitted out Gawain in the finest way possible.
First he dressed him in garments to ward off the cold,
and then in his equipment, which had been well looked
after.
Both body-armour and plate brilliantly shone
and the rings of his chainmail were rubbed free of rust.
All was clean as new, and he was duly grateful
and said thanks. 2020

He wore every piece,
attentively wiped clean,
and the finest knight in Europe
asked to be brought his horse.

He put on his magnificent clothes,
his topcoat with its emblem of the clearest design
emblazoned in velvet, with precious stones
set and sewn into it, embroidered at the seams,
and elegantly edged with most beautiful furs.
2030 But he didn't forget the girdle, the lady's gift:
Gawain remembered that in his own interests.
When he had belted his sword round his slim hips,
he wound his love-token around him twice.
So the knight neatly wrapped round his waist
the girdle of green silk, which suited him well,
so striking to see against the rich red.
But he did not wear the girdle for show –
for the display of its tassels, fine as they were,
or the glittering gold shining at its borders,
2040 but to save his skin when he'd come under attack
and face destruction without flinching, from sword
or knife.
By the time the brave man
had made his way outside,
he'd thanked more than once
all that great household.

There Gryngolet was ready, powerful and huge.
He'd been luxuriously stabled, securely minded,
so the proud horse was eager and sharp.
2050 The knight went up to him, looked at his coat
and said quietly to himself, swearing by his order:
'This is a community that cares about chivalry;
may prosperity come to that man who's their leader.
And may true love serve the lady as long as she lives.
If out of charity they so cherish a guest

and so maintain honour, may that high Lord
who rules the heaven reward them all for it.
If I am to survive any time in the world,
I'd gladly repay them, if I got the chance.'
Then he stepped on the stirrups and mounted aloft. 2060
He took on his shoulder his shield when they brought it
and spurred Gryngolet with his golden heels,
so he plunged on to the stones, no longer prancing
on one spot.
The rider on his back
bore both spear and lance.
'This castle I commend to Christ,'
was his blessing on them all.

The drawbridge was down, and the wide gates
unbarred and open to both sides. 2070
The man blessed himself quickly and crossed the
planks.
He greeted the porter, who knelt down before him,
praying good fortune for Gawain, that God should
preserve him,
and went on his way with only the guide
who was to direct him to the perilous place
where he must receive his fateful blow.
They rode through the hills, past bare branches,
climbed up the cliffs, where the cold clanged down.
The clouds were high but threatened all below.
Mist swirled on the moor and melted on the
heights. 2080
Every hill had its cover, a huge cap of mist.
The streams boiled and broke their banks,
shattering bright on the path where the two men rode
down.
Wild indeed was the way that they had to ride by,
until soon it was the hour when the sun rises
at that time of year.
They were on a high hill,

where snow lay all around;
the guide who rode beside him
2090 told Gawain to stop.

'I have got you this far, bound on this errand,
and now you are near to the notorious place
that you've asked after and sought with so much
resolve.
But I advise you honestly, since I've come to know you
and you're a mortal man for whom I've regard.
If you take my advice you'll come out of this better.
The place you are going to is known to be treacherous.
In that waste lives a man, the worst in the world;
he is powerful and forceful and likes to strike blows,
2100 and he's more huge than anyone on earth.
His body is bigger than the four strongest
in the court of King Arthur, Hector or anyone.
His principle at his Green Chapel
is that no one should pass it, however well armed,
that he doesn't kill with a blow from his hand.
For he's a ruthless man, devoid of all mercy,
whether it's priest or peasant that rides by the chapel,
monk or chaplain or anyone else.
He is as pleased to kill others as to have life himself.
2110 So I tell you, as sure as you sit in that saddle,
if you go there, you'll die, if he has his way.
You can take my word for it, if you had twenty lives
to lose.
He's lived here a long time,
with incessant violence.
You won't protect yourself
against his savage blows.

'So, good Sir Gawain, leave that knight alone
and go by some other route, for God's sake.
2120 Ride by a way where Christ may support you,
and I'll hasten home. I promise you further

that I'll swear by God and all His good
saints –
"So help me God and the relics!" and other such oaths –
that I'll protect you unwaveringly, and never say
that you ever turned to flee from anyone that I know.'
'Thank you,' said Gawain, and he spoke sharply:
'May you prosper, my friend, for wishing my welfare.
I can well believe that you'd loyally cover for me.
But however much you swore, if I escaped here,
turned and fled out of fear in the way you suggest, 2130
I'd be a cowardly knight who could not be excused.
I'll go on to the chapel, whatever may happen,
and speak to that knight what words I want,
for better or worse, as fate decrees
to have it.
Though he's a fierce fighter
to face, armed with a club,
the Lord can well dispose
to save his own servants.'

'By Our Lady,' said the guide, 'since what you say
means 2140
you want to bring destruction down on yourself
and lose your life, who am I to stop you?
Here, take your helmet, grasp your spear in your
hand
and ride down this track by the side of the rock
till you come to the depths of that wide valley.
Then look a bit to the side, to your left hand,
and you'll see in the clearing the chapel itself
and the burly warrior that holds it by force.
Now farewell in God's name, noble Sir Gawain!
For all the wealth of the world I wouldn't go with
you 2150
nor stay in your company another foot through this
forest.'
Whereupon, in the wood he turned his reins,

spurred on his horse as hard as he could
and galloped away, leaving the knight
all on his own.
'By God Himself,' said Gawain,
'I'll neither weep nor wail.
To God's will I am bound
and dedicated to Him.'

2160 Then he spurred on Gryngolet and picked up the path,
pressed on past a rock at the edge of a copse
and rode down the rough slope right to the depths.
There he looked around and saw how wild it all was,
with no sign of a refuge anywhere:
just high and steep banks, and on every side
rough gnarled crags and knuckled stones.
The clouds seemed to him to be grazed by the rocks.
He stopped and reined in his horse for a while,
looking in all directions to find the Green Chapel.
He saw nothing of the kind, which struck him as
2170 strange,
except, a little way off, a kind of a hump:
a rounded mound on the hill by the water,
near the bed of a stream that ran by there.
The water seethed in it as if it was boiling.
The knight spurred his horse and rode up to the mound,
jumped down nimbly and fastened the reins
of his fine steed to the branch of a lime tree.
Then he turned to the barrow and walked all round it,
pondering with himself what on earth it might be.
2180 It had a hole at the end and on either side,
and was covered all over with clumps of grass.
It was hollow inside, just some old cave
or a gap in an old crag. He couldn't describe it
in words.
'Well, Lord,' said the knight.
'Can this be the Green Chapel?
A place fit for the Devil
to say morning prayers at night.

'Certainly,' said Gawain, 'it's desolate round here,
an ugly oratory indeed, overgrown with weeds. 2190
It's well suited for that knight in green
to offer up his prayers to the Devil.
I'm beginning to suspect, by all my five senses,
that it's Him who has brought me here for
destruction.
It is a chapel of doom, bad luck to it!
It's the damnedest church I've ever been in!'
With his helmet on and his lance at the ready,
he climbed up to the roof of that structure.
Then he heard from a huge rock on the hillside,
from the slope across the stream, a deafening noise. 2200
Listen! It clattered on the cliff as if it would split it,
like someone edging a scythe on a stone.
Listen! It whirred and ground like water in a mill-race;
it rushed and rang, terrifying to hear.
'God!' said Gawain, 'this reception, I fancy,
is prepared in my honour, to celebrate me
properly.
God's will be done! "Alas!"ing
will do no good.
Though I'm to lose my life, 2210
no noise will make me tremble.'

Then the knight called out very loudly:
'Who's in charge of this place, to keep my appointment?
For now faithful Gawain is standing here.
If anyone wants something, let him come out at once,
now or never, and make his demand.'
'Hold on,' said someone straight over his head,
'and you will receive all I once promised you.'
He went on making that noise for a while,
turning back to his sharpening before he'd come
down. 2220
Then he appeared by a crag, coming out of a crevice,
striding from a gap with a desperate weapon,
a Danish axe ready to deliver the blow,

with its huge blade arching back to the shaft,
filed on the grindstone, four feet long.
It was that long, measured by its tassel.
And, as before, the man was all green –
face and legs, hair and beard –
except that now he travelled on foot,
2230 planking the handle on the rock and striding along.
When he got to the water, not wanting to wade,
he vaulted over on his axe and strode aggressively
with grim purpose across that wide field,
covered with snow.
Sir Gawain met the knight
without bowing too low.
The knight said, 'Good Sir,
you're a man who keeps his word.

'Gawain,' said the Green Knight, 'God preserve
you!
2240 You are very welcome to my place here.
You've timed your arrival as a true man should,
and you know the terms agreed between us:
a year back you had to take what was yours,
and I was to repay you this New Year's Day.
Here in this valley we are truly alone.
There's no one to part us – we can fight as we like.
Take off your helmet and receive what is owed;
make no more protest than I made to you
when you whipped off my head with a single stroke.'
2250 'No, by God,' said Gawain, 'who gave me my life,
I will bear you no grudge, whatever the outcome.
But keep to one stroke, while I stand my ground
and make no resistance to your doing as you like
in any way.'
He bowed his neck, bent down
and revealed the naked flesh.
He pretended to be fearless,
afraid to show his dread.

Then the man in green prepared himself quickly,
taking up his grim weapon to strike Gawain. 2260
With all the strength in his body he raised it aloft,
and swung it strongly as though he would smash him.
If it had come down the way that he brandished,
that ever-brave knight would have died from the blow.
But Gawain glanced sideways at that war-axe
as it came speeding groundwards as if to destroy him,
and with his shoulders recoiled from the steel.
The other man stopped his blade with a jerk
and protested to the knight in words of scorn.
'You can't be Gawain,' he said, 'so highly esteemed, 2270
who never feared an army on hill or in valley,
and here you are ducking before feeling a thing!
I've never heard such cowardice ascribed to him.
I neither flinched nor fled when you aimed at me,
nor made any bones about it in Arthur's court.
My head flew to my feet, yet I wasn't daunted;
and you, before any injury, cower at heart.
So I should on those grounds be declared
the better man.'
Said Gawain, 'I flinched once 2280
and won't do so again.
But if my head falls on the stones,
I can't stick it back on.

'But come on, Sir, for your reputation, finish with me.
Give me my fate and be quick about it,
for I'll stand you a stroke and recoil no more
till your axe has hit me – you have my word.'
'Here we go then,' said the knight and lifted it high,
looking as fierce as if he was mad.
He swung ferociously but did not touch him, 2290
suddenly stopping his hand before it did harm.
Gawain waited steadily, not moving a finger,
and stayed as still as a stone or tree stump
fastened to rocky ground with a hundred roots.
Then the man in green spoke out in high spirits:

'So, now you've got your courage, I must strike.
May the high order of Arthur keep you now
and save your neck in this crisis, if that is possible.'
Then Gawain furiously shouted in anger:
2300 'Oh strike away, you savage, and stop your threats;
I think it is your heart that you've instilled fear in.'
'Indeed,' said the other man, 'you speak so fiercely,
I will no longer postpone or delay your quest
at this point.'
Then he shaped up to strike,
twisting his lip and brow.
It's no wonder Gawain disliked it,
with no hope of escape.

He lifted his weapon smartly and let it fall straight
2310 with the sharp blade on the bare neck.
And hard though he struck he damaged him no more
than to nick him on the side and break the skin.
The edge cut to the muscle through the pale flesh
so the bright blood spurted past his shoulders to the
earth.
And when he saw the blood shine on the snow,
he sprang with both feet more than a spear's length,
seized hold of his helmet to put on his head,
crouched with both shoulders behind his shield,
drew out his broad sword and spoke with ferocity.
Never since he was delivered from the womb of his
2320 mother
had he felt in his lifetime half so elated.
'Stop your attack! Give no more blows!
I've taken without complaining a stroke on this ground.
And if you offer any more, I'll quickly repay it,
striking back fast – be sure about this –
and in hostility.
Just one stroke was due to me;
so our agreement was
made in Arthur's hall,
2330 so now you must stop!'

The Green Knight stood back, propped on his axe,
the handle on the ground, leaning on the blade,
and looked at the man that stood there before him,
how brave and fearless and valiantly he stood,
fully armed, undaunted. It cheered him to see it.
Then he spoke in good humour, in his booming voice
and in ringing tones said to the knight:
'My brave man, don't be so fiery here in this field.
No one has offered you any offence,
or acted outside the agreement at the king's court. 2340
I offered you a stroke. You've had it; so you're paid;
I free you of any obligation beyond that.
If I'd been hasty, I could perhaps have dealt you
a more serious blow and given cause for anger.
First I threatened you playfully with a pretend stroke
and did you no damage – offered that fairly
for the agreement we made the first night
when you kept faith with me totally
and gave me your winnings, like a good man should.
The second feint I gave for the morning 2350
when you kissed my fair wife and paid me the kisses.
For those two days I made just two gestures at you
with no harm done.
Where true men pay each other,
no one need fear foul play.
The third time though you faltered
and so you got that blow.

'For that is my garment you're wearing, that woven belt;
my wife wove it for you, that is the truth.
Now I know well your kisses and your flirting too, 2360
and the courting of my wife: I devised them myself.
I sent her to tempt you, and honestly I think
you're as faultless a man as ever drew breath.
As much as pearls surpass peas in value,
so Gawain compares to other fine knights.
But there you fell short a bit and failed in fidelity,

not from love of artwork or libidinous urges,
but because you like being alive. I don't blame you for
that!'
Gawain stood a while, frozen to the spot,
2370 so racked with remorse he inwardly shuddered;
all the blood from his heart rose to his face
as he shrank with shame at what the knight said.
Then these were the first words that came to his lips:
'A curse upon cowardice and greed just as much!
In the two of them lies villainy, the enemy of virtue.'
Then he snatched at the girdle and loosened its knot,
and violently flung it back to the knight.
'Here, take the damned thing, and bad luck go with it!
From fear of your stroke cowardice urged me
2380 to traffic in greed, forsaking my nature,
which is the generosity and loyalty pertaining to
knights.
Now I am false and at fault – I who always have
dreaded
treachery and lies. May sorrow and misery
accompany both!
I confess to you, Sir Knight,
my behaviour has been wrong.
Tell me what to do
and I will be more careful.'

Then the other man laughed and pleasantly said:
2390 'I regard as repaid any damages I suffered.
You are so fully shriven, your faults declared,
and public penance received at the point of my axe,
I declare you absolved of that guilt – as fully forgiven
as if you'd never transgressed since the day you were
born.
And I give you, Sir, the gold-bordered girdle
for it is green like my tunic. Sir Gawain,
you can think of this contest when you go forth
among noble princes, and how it is a sign
of the Green Chapel encounter of chivalrous knights.

And this New Year you must return to my house, 2400
and we'll celebrate heartily the rest of this noble
season of feasting.'
The lord embraced him closely
and said, 'We must reconcile
you with my wife,
who was your willing foe.'

'No indeed,' said the man, taking hold of his helmet
and removing it politely, thanking the knight.
'I have delayed terribly. May good fortune befall you,
and may He who confers all honours reward you! 2410
Give my respects to that paragon, your beautiful
wife –
to both of my honoured ladies, the one and the other,
that so subtly with their games have caught out their
knight.
But it's no wonder if a fool should lose his senses
and be brought to his downfall through the wiles of
women.
For Adam in this world was misled by one,
and Solomon by several, and Samson after him –
Delilah was his ruin – and David afterwards
was blinded by Bathsheba and suffered much misery.
Since all these were deluded, it would be a fine thing 2420
to love them well without trusting, if a man could
do it.
For these were the noblest of old, attended by good
fortune
beyond all the rest that lived beneath
the kingdom of heaven.
And all of them were duped
by the women they dealt with.
If I too am caught out
maybe I should be excused.

'But your girdle,' said Gawain, 'God reward you!
I will willingly wear it, not for its fine gold, 2430

nor the belt itself, nor the silk or its tassels;
not for wealth or vainglory, nor its noble working,
but as a sign of my sinfulness: that's how I'll see it
as I ride out in glory, as a reminder to me
of the frailty and weakness of the treacherous flesh,
how liable it is to the sins of impurity.
So, when pride moves in me from prowess in arms,
a glance at this love-knot will temper my ardour.
But one thing I beg, if you won't be offended:
2440 since you are the lord of that land that I stayed in
with such honour among you – may He reward you
who holds up the heaven and sits upon high –
what is your real name? Then I'll ask you no more.'
'I'll tell you that truly,' the other man said.
'Bertilak de Hautdesert I'm called in this land.
It's all through her power, Morgan Le Fay, who lives
in my house
and by well-studied arts has learned the knowledge
of wisdom, including many of the skills of Merlin,
for at one time she had dealings of love
2450 with that powerful wizard, as all your knights know
back at home.
"Morgan the goddess"
is therefore what she is called:
there's nobody so grand
that she can't get them down.

'She sent me on that errand to your noble hall
to put its pride to the test, whether it's true,
the great repute that the Round Table holds.
She sent me on this marvel to take all your wits,
2460 to scare Guinevere and cause her to die
from fear of that man who eerily spoke
with his head in his hand before the high table.
That is Morgan at my castle, the old lady.
She is your own aunt, Arthur's half-sister,
daughter of the duchess of Tintagel, on whom
noble Uther fathered Arthur, who now is so famous.

Therefore I beg you, noble Sir, come back to your aunt,
relax in my house. My whole household loves you,
and I wish you as well, on my word of honour,
as any man on earth for your great fidelity.' 2470
But he still refused him, and would assent by no means.
They embraced and kissed and commended each other
to the Prince of Paradise, and parted right there
in the cold.
Gawain on his fine steed
made haste to the king's palace,
and that knight in the pure green
wherever the whim would take him.

Along the wild roads of the land Gawain rode now
on Gryngolet, with his life restored by grace. 2480
Often he sheltered under cover and often in the open.
Many adventures he had by the way, and triumphs,
that at this time I will not go into.
The cut was healed that he'd got on his neck;
he wore the shining belt around him,
across him diagonally and tied at the side.
The lace was knotted beneath his left arm
to signal that he'd been found guilty of fault.
So the knight reached the court, all in one piece.
They were overjoyed there when the leaders learned 2490
that good Gawain was back; they thought it a blessing.
The king kissed the knight and so did the queen,
and then many true knights thronged to embrace him
and ask how he had fared. He spoke of strange things,
telling of all he'd had to endure:
the trial of the chapel, the Green Knight's nature,
the love of the lady, and lastly the girdle.
He showed them the neck wound, fully exposed,
which he'd endured at the knight's hand because of his
deception,
to his disgrace. 2500
He suffered in the telling,
groaned in grief and anger.

The blood rose to his face
with shame when he showed his wound.

'Look, Lord,' said the man as he fingered the girdle,
'Here's the band of blame like the one on my neck:
the injury and failing that I have succumbed to
out of the cowardice and greed that I displayed there.
It's the mark of untruth that I was caught out in,
2510 and I must wear it as long as I live.
Though a man may hide his crime, if it's not exposed,
once it is there it will never be gone.'
The king cheered the knight up, and all the court too
laughed loudly about it, and formally agreed
that all lords and ladies of the Round Table,
every member of that fellowship, would wear such a
belt,
a bright green sash worn crosswise about them,
and they'd wear it so in solidarity with Gawain.
For it was reckoned to be to the Round Table's credit,
2520 and the man who would wear it honoured for ever,
as is declared in the finest book of romance.
Well, such was this adventure in the days of King
Arthur,
which the book of the Britons gives evidence of.
After Brutus, that brave man, came over here first
when the siege and the battle were over at Troy
long ago.
Before now, many wonders
have happened much like this.
May He who wore the crown of thorns
2530 bring us to his bliss! Amen.

HONY SOYT QUI MAL PENCE

Notes

Line numbers are in most cases correct for both the translation and the original and are used for reference here. For a fuller set of annotations, based on the original text of the poem, see T. Silverstein, *Sir Gawain and the Green Knight: A New Critical Edition* (University of Chicago Press, 1984).

1. *When the war and the siege of Troy were all over*: The poem, like *Pearl* in the same manuscript and generally thought to be by the same poet, begins and ends with the same reference, to the aftermath of the siege of Troy (see l. 2525). Among the European nations founded in legend by descendants of the Trojans are the Britons, established by the grandson or great-grandson of Aeneas, called Brutus (ll. 5–15). From him the eponymous name 'Brut' was applied to mythological treatments of the political origins of Britain, notably in the twelfth-century poems Wace's *Roman de Brut* (*c.* 1155) and Laghamon's *Brut* (*c.* 1200), in Anglo-Norman and West-Midlands English respectively.

3. *the man who'd betrayed it*: Normally Antenor (as in Chaucer's contemporary *Troilus and Criseyde*). But there was a strong medieval tradition of Aeneas as co-betrayer with Antenor, and the syntax of line 5 of this poem ('Then the noble Aeneas') means that the reference in line 3 could be to Aeneas.

11. *Ticius*: The name Ticius is not otherwise known and it has been variously emended. However, this list of eponymous founders is not historically persuasive anyway.

13. *illustrious Brutus*: See note to line 1 above. In the original text, he is called *Felix* ('happy or fortunate', which I have translated as 'illustrious'), and this may be a corruption of some other Latin term, *silvius* or *filius*. It has also been suggested that the appellation was ironic, and that this legendary Brutus was notoriously ill famed. Whatever the origin, it is possible that it is this

'happy' ancestry that causes Arthur to be oddly characterized as 'joly of his joyfnes' (literally 'gay in his youth') in line 86.

33–6. *exactly as passed down . . . down all the days*: It has usually been thought that the reference in this wheel ('exactly as passed down' ('with lel letters loken': literally 'secured with the right letters')) refers to the metrical form, with both verbs in line 33 – 'stad' and 'stoken' – meaning 'set down', perhaps implying conformity with the alliterative tradition.

39. *the famous company of the whole Round Table*: This is the first reference to the Round Table in the poem. The term is used again by the Green Knight at line 313, but it seems to be institutional rather than descriptive because the company is organized hierarchically: there is a 'dece' ('top table', l. 61) and a 'hyghe table' ('high table', l. 108).

44. *Celebrations continued the whole of a fortnight*: Editors have occasionally worried about the original's 'fifteen days' that the Christmas celebrations are said to have lasted, rather than the traditional twelve. But it is probably an approximate term, like 'fortnight', which I have used to translate it here. See note to l. 1022.

86. *he was so young and impulsive – you might call him boyish*: This line has been much discussed because the term 'childgered' (boyish) might seem to imply a light-mindedness in Arthur, perhaps mirrored by the court's failure to take Gawain's experience seriously at the end (see note to l. 2513). But the light-heartedness of Arthur and his court might just as well be seen as a courtly virtue, a kind of *sprezzatura*.

90–99. *He had another ritual . . . which of them fortune would favour*: Arthur's practice of not eating before he has witnessed or heard of a marvel is paralleled in several romances, including the Carados episode in the *First Continuation of Chrétien's Perceval*, which is one of the closest parallels to the decapitation bargain. The noise all hear (l. 132) liberates the king to sit at the table because it portends the marvel he has been waiting for.

109. *Noble Sir Gawain sat next to the queen*: Gawain is here linked with Guinevere, both at the table and by alliteration. Their connection has been seen as significant because the Green Knight explains at the end – somewhat unconvincingly – that the gruesome events that follow were devised by Morgan Le Fay to frighten Guinevere to death. The spelling of the queen's name is remarkably various through the poem: 'Guenore', 'Gwenore', 'Gaynour', 'Guenever' and 'Wenore'. It was suggested by Theo-

dore Silverstein that the spelling 'Wenore' (l. 945) makes possible a particularly effective use of the rhetorical figure called *traductio*, which employs two words of similar form but different meaning: the lady in Bertilak's castle strikes Gawain as 'wener than Wenore' ('more beautiful than Guinevere'). Gawain's name varies similarly throughout the poem and has the same fluctuation between an initial 'G' or 'W', which is exploited for alliterative flexibility. It is familiar to us as the French/English/Welsh variation in the same name: Guillaume/William/Gwilym.

136. *when a monstrous apparition strode in the door*: The verb for the Green Knight's approach in the original is 'hales', which has an air of informality that establishes his intrusion as cheerfully indifferent to courtly protocol.

150. *he was green from head to toe*: The narrative is at pains to emphasize that the knight and his horse are coloured green, not just in green armour, which is what 'the green knight' would normally mean.

157. *Neat, tight stockings of the same colour*: The line in the original ('Heme, wel-haled hose of that same grene') lacks alliteration in the second half. Several editors supply 'hewe' to emend it, and I have translated this as 'colour'.

160. *shoeless*: The fact that this powerful intruder has no armed shoes is taken as an indication of non-violent intentions. However, occasionally, the word in the original, 'scholes', has been interpreted as a noun describing the kind of shoes he is wearing.

206–7. *But in one hand he had a bough of holly . . . when groves are bare*: The Green Knight's holly, the midwinter tree, is one of the pieces of evidence used by the 'anthropological critics' (see Introduction here, p. xvii) to see the subliminal meaning of the poem as an allegory of the change of the seasons. The Green Knight, symbolizing the old year, has his head cut off by the young sun-god Gawain (who is associated with the 'young blood' of Arthur and his court in line 89), to renew the yearly cycle.

296. *in return*: This bob 'in return' translates the original's word 'barlay', which is usually compared to the truce-word 'barley', still used in children's games in the north of England. Its origin is obscure.

298. *of one year and a day*: The interim of a year and a day occurs commonly in romances and fairy tales. In this poem, and in *Pearl*, it seems to have a formal echo in the organization into 101 stanzas.

304. *and scarily glared round with his red eyes*: The word I have

translated as 'scarily' is 'runischly' in the original, a word that occurs in several poems of the northern alliterative revival and in two other poems in this manuscript. Its origin is obscure, but it clearly means something like 'ferociously'. It is applied to the Green Knight's actions again at line 457: 'With a violent tug he pulled the reins round'.

379–81. *But first let me ask you . . . I am called Gawain*: If 'trawthe', fidelity to one's word, is the central virtue in the poem, Gawain manifests it strikingly by the readiness with which he declares his identity, by contrast with the Green Knight, who remains a nameless figure of mystery.

455. *so, if you ask, you won't fail to find me*: The Green Knight's claim that those who seek him cannot fail to find him gives him perhaps a sinister connotation of the figure of Death, the only thing that seekers always find, as in Chaucer's *The Pardoner's Tale*.

477. *hang up your axe*: An idiom in Middle English which means 'Stop what you are doing'. But it is typical of the defamiliarizing of the proverbial favoured by this poet, as in the famous phrase 'You are welcome to my body' (l. 1237). Gawain, of course, is literally laying his axe aside.

499. *the end rarely matches the spirit it starts in*: This is one of several aphorisms that Theodore Silverstein, one of the poem's best editors and critics, says is typical of the poet's learned borrowings from Cicero and other wisdom texts, such as the Old Testament. Silverstein says this line translates Cato's *Distychs*, Book I, l. 18 (though other editors dispute the exactness of the reference). In the context this ominous passage should alert us to the unpredictable course the story will take.

500–531. *Yuletide is past and the New Year is too . . . ever the same*: This description of the changing of the seasons, a *cursus annorum* ('courses of the year'), is one of the most admired passages in the poem. *So the year passes on through its series of yesterdays*: The plural of 'yesterdays' inevitably reminds the modern reader of Macbeth's 'And all our yesterdays have lighted fools / The way to dusty death' (Act V, scene v); and, although the idea of past yesterdays is a commonplace in medieval literature, this is a rare instance of the adverb 'yesterday' taking a plural 's' like a noun.

567. *asked for his armour, which duly was brought*: The hero's arming is an important set piece in English literature from *Beowulf* onwards. It is striking that in Gawain's case the stress is on display and opulence more than on protection (ll. 568–91).

597. *Gryngolet*: 'Gryngolet', or a form like it, was the name of Gawain's horse from Chrétien de Troyes's *Yvain* (*c.* 1170) onwards. Its origin is probably Celtic.

605. *Then Gawain fervently kissed his helmet*: Gawain's kissing his helmet has a liturgical air to it – like the priest's kissing his stole when robing for Mass.

620. *the pentangle engraved in bright gold colours*: The pentangle as the symbol of Gawain's interlinked virtues (ll. 625–35) is unique to this poem, and the word is peculiar to English. The interdependence of the five virtues is the crucial point; failure in any one of them means failure in all. Gawain is perfect or he is nothing. None of the twenty-five qualities in the five groups of five emerges as particularly distinctive. Organization into fives – into 'quincunxes' – was a popular practice, most famously discussed in Sir Thomas Browne's *The Garden of Cyrus* (1658). Browne's *Pseudodoxia Epidemica* ('*Vulgar Errors*', 1646) features the next occurrence of the word in English. The flawlessness of the pearl in the poem *Pearl* similarly signifies unbreakable perfection, and Gawain's superior integrity is compared to the pearl at the end of this poem (ll. 2363–4).

626. *to represent truth in balance with justice*: It is sometimes claimed that 'truth', fidelity to his word, is Gawain's distinctive virtue (see note to lines 379–81 above). But the word is perhaps too general to be distinctive – rather like 'goodness'. It is the central virtue in Chaucer's *The Franklin's Tale* ('Trouthe is the hyeste thing that man may kepe': *The Canterbury Tales*, V, l. 1479 (all references to *The Canterbury Tales* are to the Riverside edition)), and the quality Chaucer's Criseyde most values in Troilus ('moral virtue founded upon Truth': *Troilus and Criseyde*, Book IV, l. 1672).

629–30. *It is called . . . 'the endless knot', in all parts of England*: In fact, there is no evidence that it was called 'the endless knot' in any part of England, any more than that it was called 'The pure pentangle' (l. 664). The poet is inventing a tradition.

644–50. *And whenever this knight . . . his heart would not falter*: Gawain is Mary's knight because he has taken a vow of chastity – to be faithful to her – and her image inside his shield balances the courtly virtues of the pentangle. The five joys in Christ taken by Mary are most familiar as the five joyful mysteries of the rosary: the Annunciation, the Visitation, the Nativity, the Presentation in the Temple and the Finding in the Temple. In fact it was Arthur who was more often associated with Mary. In this poem many people swear colloquially by Mary, including the guide who directs Gawain to the Green Knight (l. 2140).

674–83. *By Christ, it's a pity . . . some silly competition such as knights have at Christmas*: This lament for the reckless loss of a great knight is paralleled in several of the *Gawain* analogues, especially in *Le chevalier à l'epée* in L. E. Brewer, '*Sir Gawain and the Green Knight*': *Sources and Analogues*, p. 111.

689–90. *Many a wild road . . . as the book reports*: Reference to the report of an authoritative book is a standard feature of romances, in English most familiar in Sir Thomas Malory's *Le Morte D'Arthur* (*c.* 1469).

691–702. *While this hero rode through the whole of England . . . or by men of goodwill*: Gawain's arduous journey through this winter landscape is admired for its tactile evocativeness, and for its surprisingly real references to places in North Wales and northern England. These localizations seem to pull the romantic story into a real world. As John Burrow puts it (*A Reading of Sir Gawain*), a knight who passes your back door seems more likely to fail in his quest.

720–23. *At times he fought dragons . . . giants who stalked him from the fells above*: The opponents are despatched with summary alliteration ('bulls and bears and boars'), and the giants and 'trolls of the forest' (Ted Hughes's 'wodwos' (in the original Middle English, 'wood-kernes')) seem to offer little real threat. It is again typical of the poem's realism that 'the winter was worse' (l. 726) than the creatures he has to fight. Gawain is 'Nearly killed by the sleet' (l. 729).

764–70. *before he saw, in the wood, a moated dwelling . . . surrounded by trees for two miles and more*: The topography of the area around Bertilak's castle has been interestingly localized north of Leek, on the Staffordshire–Cheshire border. See Ralph Elliott, 'Landscape and Geography' in Brewer and Gibson, *Companion*, pp. 105–17.

774. *Saint Julian*: Saint Julian the Hospitaller ('Gilyan' in the original) is much invoked in the Middle Ages as the patron saint of travellers.

787–802. *The walls went a great depth down . . . it looked as if it was cut out of paper*: Although the shining castle looks as if it is 'cut out of paper', it is a solid evocation of a fourteenth-century castle, and it has been linked to Beeston Castle in Cheshire (see Michael Thompson, 'Castles' in Brewer and Gibson, *Companion*, pp. 119–30). It has generally been assumed recently that the poet came from somewhere around Cheshire, and that his knowledge of French romance and cosmopolitanism may be linked to the presence of courtiers from his native Cheshire at the court of Richard II in the 1390s. See the excellent introduction by Helen Cooper to the verse translation of the poem by Keith Harrison (Oxford, 1998).

813–37. *By Saint Peter, I will . . . to your heart's content*: The extravagant politeness of Gawain's reception is in marked contrast to the exchanges at the arrival of the Green Knight at Camelot.

866–8. *He seemed in appearance to everyone there . . . the most glowing and brilliant colours*: Gawain is like a vision of spring in his rich colours. This line is often quoted by exponents of the 'anthropological approach', seeing the poem as rooted in a mythic story about the succession – and overthrow – of winter by spring.

897. *penitential fare*: This elaborate meal of fish dishes is 'penitential' because on Christmas Eve it is still Advent, a penitential period. The real Christmas fare will begin the next day.

916–27. *Now we will see refinement in practice . . . learn all about love-talking*: This court's expectation of Gawain is that he will be the pre-eminent courtly lover. But they see his appearance among them too as a Christmas gift from God (l. 920), in conformity with the ambiguity of the courtly lover's status as both secular lover and Christian hero. Gawain's continental courtliness is stressed in these episodes; compare the 'Frenkysh fare' ('French manners') at line 1116.

928–69. *By the time dinner was over . . . was her companion for sure*: This is the longest stanza in the poem, over three times as long as the shortest (ll. 20–36). But no interpretative significance has been convincingly argued for the differing lengths of the main part of the stanzas.

945. *more beautiful than Guinevere*: 'Wener than Wenore' in the original, this is an instance of a kind of punning that the poem favours. Gawain's reflection that this lady is more beautiful than the queen might sound rather ungallant, coming from this model of knightly fair-speaking. It indicates, of course, that Guinevere is the measure of female beauty. Perhaps more importantly, it will emerge at the end of the poem that Guinevere's enemy, Morgan Le Fay, has conjured up the poem's events to frighten Guinevere to death. Perhaps the lord's wife surpassing Guinevere in beauty is part of the scheme, as in the story of *Snow White*. See note to l. 109 above.

950. *These ladies were very unalike in appearance*: The contrast between the young and old ladies also sounds ungallant, and the description of the older lady in the wheel at the end of this stanza – 'Her body was short and fat, / her buttocks spreading wide' (ll. 966–7) – is foreign to the prevailing courtly tone. Like several things in the poem, it fits the anthropological Old Year/New Year theme well. In any case, 'the loathly lady' is a common figure in medieval narratives, as in Chaucer's *The Wife of Bath's Tale*.

1022. *Saint John's Day*: The Feast of Saint John the Evangelist falls on 27 December. It has often been noted that the poem loses one day between Christmas and New Year, as it proceeds day by day from 28 December to New Year in three days instead of four. Such an omission would not normally merit mention in romance; the fact that it is noted at all is, paradoxically, testimony to the unusual expectations of realism this poem sets up. See note to l. 44 above.

1105. *One more thing . . . let's make an agreement*: The second story-line, 'the exchange of winnings', starts here. Close as the analogues to *Gawain* are in some respects, no other text links the 'exchange of winnings' storyline with that of the 'beheading test'. The linking is done remarkably seamlessly. Recent criticism has stressed how much the exchange is couched in official-sounding commercial terms. See ll. 1938–41.

1145. *so the story says*: This (in the original 'as I haf herde telle') is a common formula in romances and ballads. But we should not assume that the poet is referring to a particular source. (See also note to ll. 689–90.)

1150–77. *At the first sound of the hunt . . . right to the fall of night*: Within the framing context of the beheading bargain, physical violence has particular force in this poem. The horrific description of the killing of animals here has a power rarely paralleled in medieval English: 'crazy with fear . . . They screamed and they bled and they died on the hills'. It seems particularly pointed by contrast with the lord's reaction to the hunting, which makes him 'delirious with delight' (l. 1174). The close season, when it was prohibited to kill the male deer, ran from 14 September to 20 June.

1182–94. *As he dozed there in peace . . . to see if he'd wake up*: The suggestive stealthiness of the lady's approach to Gawain's bedside shows the poet's powers of tactile description at their most impressive.

1210–11. *Unless there's a truce . . . you can be sure*: The lady uses the terminology of siege warfare, hinting at Gawain's greater physical strength. He attempts to bring the exchange back to courtly decorum, culminating in his declaration that he is her 'humble servant' and she is his 'ruler', praying 'May Christ reward you!' (ll. 1278–9).

1237. *You are welcome to my body*: In this declaration, 'my body' can idiomatically mean 'my person' in general terms (as Chaucer's Shipman seems to refer to himself as 'my joly body' (*The Canterbury Tales*, II, l. 1185)). But it remains a disconcertingly literal remark in the situation in Gawain's bedroom. Gawain's courtly offer of 'service in word or in *deed*' (l. 1246, my italics) is similarly compromised by the bedroom setting.

1263. *Madame . . . may Our Lady reward you*: Side by side with the terms of seduction and courtliness, Gawain and the lady contrive to declare fidelity to Gawain's patron, Mary, 'Our Lady' (see also l. 1268).

1293. *but that you are Gawain can not be believed*: The lady's repeated charge that this cannot be Gawain (see l. 1481, and the Green Knight's similar doubts at l. 2270) almost changes the name into a quality. He is a classic romance hero in his wish to live up to his name. It is highly significant that we never learn the name of 'the lady', vividly as she is evoked. As in the major poems of courtly love, such as those of the troubadours, she remains the *donna*, 'the lady'.

1296. *The lady blessed him*: The verb 'blessed' means 'reassured, wished well'. But I have kept the word from the original to sustain the pseudo-religious language of courtly love.

1319–57. *All this time, the lord was at his sport . . . by the four hocks*: Skill in 'venery', hunting and the division of the quarry, was an aristocratic accomplishment, described in medieval / Renaissance handbooks such as George Gascoigne's *The Noble Arts of Venerie or Hunting* (1575), and attested in many romances such as *Sir Tristrem* (*c.* 1300). Tristan was a particularly admired exponent of this art. *raven's portion*: The raven's portion (or Bone), the 'corbeles fee', is a recurrent requirement in the hunting manuals.

1412. *By the time that the cock had clarioned three times*: It is hard to exclude the association of Peter's betrayal of Christ from the cock's threefold crowing, particularly given the call to Mass here, but it probably only means a repeated alarm.

1434–6. *The hunt ringed the crag and the thicket beside it . . . what beast it was that the bloodhounds had scented*: The identity of this second beast is held back for suspense. The boar is the most noble of the hunted beasts, probably because of its greater strength as an adversary. Here it is the most formidable opponent for the lord, and the one that he fights finally in single combat (ll. 1581–96). Although there is an obvious general comparison to be made between the hunting of the beasts and the tempting of Gawain, there doesn't seem to be a day-for-day correspondence. The battle put up by the single boar, separated from the rest of the herd (the 'sounder' in the original text, l. 1440), against forty hounds, is unmistakably heroic (ll. 1437–53).

1644. *Saint Giles*: Saint Giles (Aegidius) was a hermit of Provence who died *c.* 710. He was very popular in the Middle Ages. It is striking that one of the best-known stories about him tells of his being wounded by an arrow. It was shot by King Wamba at a female deer which had taken refuge with the saint.

1679–80. *I've tested you twice ... "Third is final"*: The Norse-derived verb in the original, 'fraysted' ('tested'), means 'asked' or 'made trial of': a sinister term in what is supposed to be a friendly game. The following line's proverb 'Third is final', or 'Third time pays for all', is similarly disquieting.

1699–1700. *Some came on the path ... with his instinctive wiles*: The fact that the quarry in the final hunt is the less aggressive or exalted (in the hierarchy of hunted beasts) fox is typical of the poem's inclination to belie expectation. The fox is tricky, rather than strong.

1725–8. *He was threatened ... so wily was Reynard*: Fox hunts, which are dealt with in the handbooks of venery, are less common in the romance than in more homely narratives such as the beast-fable of Chaucer's *The Nun's Priest's Tale*, in which the fox's pursuers make a great racket, crying 'Ha! Ha! the fox!' (*The Canterbury Tales*, VII, l. 3381).

1733–4. *But love would not let ... that stirred in her heart*: The lady cannot sleep because of her love for Gawain, a condition that usually applies to the lovelorn male in medieval texts. It raises the interesting question of whether she really is smitten with Gawain or just playing her role. She is certainly exercising her arts of seduction to the full, 'her upper body bare at the front and the back' (l. 1741). Likewise, the fact that Gawain's heart 'swelled with surging joy' (l. 1762) when he sees her suggests that he too is amorously driven. The circumstances are perilous: in moral terms, it is potentially 'an occasion of sin', in which Mary keeps Gawain under her protection (l. 1769).

1750–54. *In heavy troubled sleep . . . without resistance*: Gawain's fear at the prospect of decapitation disturbs his sleep, once again giving an impression of remarkably modern psychological reality, far removed from the suspension of reality that traditionally characterizes the romance. This realistic dreaming is stressed by another of the poem's leading critics, A. C. Spearing, in *The Gawain-poet* (Cambridge, 1970).

1773–5. *He was worried for his chivalry . . . good lord whose castle it was*: These lines summarize succinctly Gawain's dilemma, which is the central question raised in the poem: can he be perfectly courteous with the lady and at the same time virtuously loyal to his host, her husband?

1790–91. *I swear I have . . . for some time*: It is not obvious why Gawain is confident that he won't have a sweetheart for some time to come.

1830. *And quickly she took off the belt from her waist*: Given her *déshabillé*, the girdle which she offers is clearly highly suggestive. In the original the word I have translated as 'waist' is 'sydes' (sides), which were one of the standard elements in the listing of feminine erotic features. It is notable that, among the six Eucharistic vestments recognized by the medieval Catholic Church, the girdle was said to symbolize freedom from sexual desire.

1866–9. *He thanked her very warmly . . . for a third time*: Gawain's acceptance of the girdle is the moment of betrayal, perhaps symbolized by the three kisses, recalling the cock's threefold crowing in line 1412. Betrayal by a kiss recalls for us Judas's identification of Jesus with a kiss to the soldiers who came to arrest him, as in George Herbert's 'The Sacrifice' (1633): 'Judas, dost thou betray me with a kiss?'

1880–82. *Then he confessed clearly . . . asking the priest for complete absolution*: There has been much discussion about the efficacy of Gawain's confession. If he confesses that he has kept the girdle, in contravention of the agreement with his host, he would have to return it before getting absolution. However, this seems to be interpreting the episode as an instance of theft as sin more explicitly than the poem does; in any case, he has not yet failed to give it back at this point! It remains striking that the Green Knight's final judgement on Gawain is expressed in the terms of penance, suggesting that Gawain is absolved at last: 'You are so fully shriven, your faults declared, / and public penance received at the point of my axe' (ll. 2391–2). In the present confession, he has 'penance in full and was shriven as clear / as if the Day of

Judgement was fixed for next morning' (ll. 1883–4). For Gawain, of course, judgement *will* come the next morning.

1915–17. *They raised the liveliest baying ... with hue and cry*: Prayers for the soul of Reynard are a standard feature of fox hunts in medieval stories and in ballads. This may link with the notion of forgiveness of sin in Gawain.

1938–41. *By God ... the debt that I owed is openly paid*: Again the exchanges between the lord and Gawain are described in commercial terms. The kisses are 'merchandise', paid for at 'a price'. See note to line 1105.

1964. *I pledge myself in exchange for one of your men*: Gawain's offering of himself in exchange for the services of one of the lord's men as guide is hard to understand fully. It is probably an elegant formula of politeness.

1998–2008. *Now the New Year's approaching ... he knew well the time*: The last of the poem's four sections as they are conventionally agreed begins with another great set piece of winter weather, coinciding with Gawain's anxious insomnia (ll. 2007–8).

2033. *he wound his love-token around him twice*: It might seem odd that Gawain wraps the girdle, the lady's love-token, around him where it is clearly visible against 'the rich red' of his armour. Presumably he doesn't expect to see the lord again, who would recognize his lady's gift to Gawain.

2054. *And may true love serve the lady as long as she lives*: Gawain's wish that true love should serve the lady recalls the wish that true love should attend Gawain after he has taken the girdle (l. 1893). It does not seem to be expected here that courtly love should be permanently directed towards the same person.

2118–19. *So, good Sir Gawain . . . some other route, for God's sake*: The temptation of Gawain by the guide, urging him to break his agreement with the Green Knight, has associations with the tempting of Christ by Satan in disguise. Gawain's trust in God is the appropriate Christian response (ll. 2138–9; ll. 2157–8).

2172. *a rounded mound on the hill by the water*: There is a marked contrast between the expectations raised by the French word 'chapel' (l. 2186) and the primitive 'balgh bergh bi a bonke' ('rounded mound on a hill') which Gawain sees. It is 'nobot an olde cave' ('just some old cave', l. 2182).

2219–20. *He went on making that noise . . . before he'd come down*: The Green Knight's assiduous sharpening of his axe is a fine melodramatic detail.

2270. *You can't be Gawain*: The Green Knight's declaration that Gawain's flinching must mean he is not really Gawain recalls the lady's similar doubts about his identity as courteous lover (ll. 1293, 1481).

2366–8. *But there you fell short . . . I don't blame you for that*: The Green Knight's forgiveness of a sin committed out of love of life has been much invoked by the anthropological critics who believe he is a vegetative life force.

2400–2402. *And this New Year . . . season of feasting*: The invitation to return to his house to celebrate New Year raises the question of the 'real' identity of the Green Knight / lord of the castle. At the end he rides off 'wherever the whim would take him' (l. 2478). But before that, he has, finally, told Gawain his name, Bertilak (or Bercilak) de Hautdesert (l. 2445). Earlier versions of the name are not known, though there is a figure called 'Berthelai' in the romance *Lancelot du Lac*. For a discussion of these two rather obscure, French-derived name elements, 'Bertilak' and 'Hautdesert', see Derek Brewer's 'Some names' in Brewer and Gibson, *Companion*.

2414–28. *But it's no wonder . . . maybe I should be excused*: Gawain's conventional and graceless attribution of his failings to the wiles of women, citing biblical precedent, is oddly conventional in this narrative, which challenges convention so often.

2446. *It's all through her power, Morgan Le Fay*: The explanation that the whole plot was conjured up by Morgan Le Fay to frighten Guinevere to death (see note on l. 945, 'Wener than Wenore') is not very persuasive. It was elegantly dismissed by John Spiers as 'a bone for the rationalizing mind to play with, and be kept quiet with'. The way the knight explains who Morgan is in relation to Arthur (ll. 2464–6), as well as her role in the plot, has the air of a footnote.

2487–8. *The lace was knotted . . . found guilty of fault*: It is clear enough that Gawain now wears the girdle as the mark of his fault. It is not clear whether his wearing it on his left side in particular has any sinister association.

2494–2512. *He spoke of strange things . . . it will never be gone*: The debriefing of a knight at the end of a quest, outlining his experiences to Arthur, is a standard feature. In this case it is unusually anguishing.

2513–21. *The king cheered the knight up . . . in the finest book of romance*: The poem leaves us with three judgements on Gawain: his own sense of failure by the standards of perfection; the Green

Knight's partial retribution; and the laughter of the court which seems to hark back to the light-mindedness of Arthur and his entourage at the beginning (see notes to ll. 13 and 86 above). The 'finest book of romance' seems to see the girdle as a badge of honour.

2523–6. *which the book of the Britons . . . long ago*: The poem circles back to the 'Brutus bokes' and the Trojan reference of the opening. The French motto of the Order of the Garter has been added at the end of the manuscript. It was founded by Edward III in 1348, and has no obvious bearing on this poem, which, at least in this written form, is agreed to be of later origin. Edward III did take an oath at a great tournament in Windsor in 1344 that he would follow in Arthur's footsteps and create a Round Table for his knights.

Appendix: Original text of lines 1998–2024

Any modern spelling of a medieval manuscript has to be inadequate in many ways. What I have done here is to replace two obsolete consonants ‘þ’ and ‘ȝ’ by ‘th’ and ‘gh’ (sometimes ‘y’) respectively. I have used ‘u’ and ‘v’ with their modern values (that of vowel and consonant), rather than abiding by the medieval manuscript practice of using ‘v’ for both vowel and consonant at the start of words and ‘u’ for both in the middle of words. I have replaced the final ‘z’ (for plural nouns and the third person singular of verbs) with the modern ‘s’. My hope is that what remains will give a sense of what the original language sounded like, especially in its ringing consonants. I have kept a caesura throughout to indicate the important break between the first and second half-lines. You will find the translation of this passage of the text on pp. 63–4.

Now neghes the New Yere,   and the nyght passes,
The day dryves to the derk,   as Dryghtyn* biddes.
Bot wylde wederes of the worlde   wakened theroute.   2000
Clowdes kesten kenly   the colde to the erthe,
With nyghe innoghe of the northe   the naked to tene.*
The snawe snitered ful snart,   that snayped* the wylde.
The werbelande wynde   wapped* from the hyghe
And drof uche* dale   ful of dryftes ful grete.
The leude* lystened ful wel   that ley in his bedde.
Thagh he lowkes* his liddes   ful lyttel he slepes.
Bi uch cok that crue   he knwe wel the steven.*

* *Dryghtyn*: the Lord   * *to tene*: to pain, annoy
* *snayped*: shivered, nipped   * *wapped*: warbled, whipped
* *uche*: each   * *leude*: man   * *lowkes*: shuts   * *steven*: hour

Deliverly he dressed up er the day sprenged,
2010 For there was lyght of a laumpe that lemed* in his chambre.
He called to his chamberlayn that cofly* hym swared,*
And bede hym bryng hym his bruny* and his blonk* sadel.
That other ferkes* hym up and feches hym his wedes,
And graythes* me Sir Gawayn upon a great wyse.
Fyrst he clad hym in his clothes the colde for to were,*
And sythen* his other harnays* that holdely* was keped,
Bothe his paunce* and his plates, piked ful clene,
The rynges rokked* of the roust of his riche bruny.
And al was fresch as upon fyrst, and he was fayn thenne
2020 To thonk*.
He hade upon uche pece
Wypped* ful wel and wlonk.*
The gayest into Grece,
The burne bede bryng his blonk.*

* *lemed*: shone * *cofly*: quickly * *swared*: answered
* *bruny*: mail shirt * *blonk*: horse * *ferkes*: rises
* *graythes*: prepares * *were*: guard against * *sythen*: next
* *harnays*: harness * *holdely*: carefully * *paunce*: body-armour
* *rokked*: rubbed free * *thonk*: say thanks * *Wypped*: wiped
* *wlonk*: nobly * *blonk*: horse

read more

PENGUIN CLASSICS

THE EPIC OF GILGAMESH

'Surpassing all other kings, heroic in stature,
brave scion of Uruk, wild bull on the rampage!
Gilgamesh the tall, magnificent and terrible'

Miraculously preserved on clay tablets dating back as much as four thousand years, the poem of Gilgamesh, king of Uruk, is the world's oldest epic, predating Homer by many centuries. The story tells of Gilgamesh's adventures with the wild man Enkidu, and of his arduous journey to the ends of the earth in quest of the Babylonian Noah and the secret of immortality. Alongside its themes of family, friendship and the duties of kings, *The Epic of Gilgamesh* is, above all, about mankind's eternal struggle with the fear of death.

The Babylonian version has been known for over a century, but linguists are still deciphering new fragments in Akkadian and Sumerian. Andrew George's gripping translation brilliantly combines these into a fluent narrative and will long rank as the definitive English *Gilgamesh*.

'This masterly new verse translation' *The Times*

Translated with an introduction by Andrew George

www.penguin.com

read more

PENGUIN CLASSICS

THE ILIAD HOMER

'Look at me. I am the son of a great man. A goddess was my mother. Yet death and inexorable destiny are waiting for me'

One of the foremost achievements in Western literature, Homer's *Iliad* tells the story of the darkest episode in the Trojan War. At its centre is Achilles, the greatest warrior-champion of the Greeks, and his refusal to fight after being humiliated by his leader Agamemnon. But when the Trojan Hector kills Achilles's close friend Patroclus, he storms back into battle to take revenge – although knowing this will ensure his own early death. Interwoven with this tragic sequence of events are powerfully moving descriptions of the ebb and flow of battle, of the domestic world inside Troy's besieged city of Ilium, and of the conflicts between the gods on Olympus as they argue over the fate of mortals.

E. V. Rieu's acclaimed translation of Homer's *Iliad* was one of the first titles published in Penguin Classics, and now has classic status itself. For this edition, Rieu's text has been revised, and a new introduction and notes by Peter Jones complement the original introduction.

Translated by E. V. Rieu
Revised and updated by Peter Jones with D. C. H. Rieu
Edited with an introduction and notes by Peter Jones

www.penguin.com

read more

PENGUIN CLASSICS

BEOWULF

'With bare hands shall I
grapple with the fiend, fight to the death here,
hater and hated! He who is chosen
shall deliver himself to the Lord's judgement'

Beowulf is the greatest surviving work of literature in Old English, unparalleled in its epic grandeur and scope. It tells the story of the heroic Beowulf and of his battles, first with the monster Grendel, who has laid waste to the great hall of the Danish king Hrothgar, then with Grendel's avenging mother, and finally with a dragon that threatens to devastate his homeland. Through its blend of myth and history, *Beowulf* vividly evokes a twilight world in which men and supernatural forces live side by side, and celebrates the endurance of the human spirit in a transient world.

Michael Alexander's landmark modern English verse translation has been revised to take account of new readings and interpretations. His new introduction discusses central themes of *Beowulf* and its place among epic poems, the history of its publication and reception, and issues of translation.

'A foundation stone of poetry in English' Andrew Motion

Translated with an introduction and notes by Michael Alexander

www.penguin.com

read more

PENGUIN CLASSICS

THE FAERIE QUEENE EDMUND SPENSER

'Great Lady of the greatest Isle, whose light
Like Phoebus lampe throughout the world doth shine'

The Faerie Queene was one of the most influential poems in the English language. Dedicating his work to Elizabeth I, Spenser brilliantly united Arthurian romance and Italian renaissance epic to celebrate the glory of the Virgin Queen. Each book of the poem recounts the quest of a knight to achieve a virtue: the Red Crosse Knight of Holinesse, who must slay a dragon and free himself from the witch Duessa; Sir Guyon, Knight of Temperance, who escapes the Cave of Mammon and destroys Acrasia's Bowre of Bliss; and the lady-knight Britomart's search for her Sir Artegall, revealed to her in an enchanted mirror. Although composed as a moral and political allegory, *The Faerie Queene*'s magical atmosphere captivated the imaginations of later poets from Milton to the Victorians.

This edition includes the letter to Raleigh, in which Spenser declares his intentions for his poem, the commendatory verses by Spenser's contemporaries and his dedicatory sonnets to the Elizabethan court, and is supplemented by a table of dates and a glossary.

Edited by Thomas P. Roche, Jr, with C. Patrick O'Donnell, Jr

www.penguin.com

THE STORY OF PENGUIN CLASSICS

Before 1946 ... 'Classics' are mainly the domain of academics and students, without readable editions for everyone else. This all changes when a little-known classicist, E. V. Rieu, presents Penguin founder Allen Lane with the translation of Homer's *Odyssey* that he has been working on and reading to his wife Nelly in his spare time.

1946 *The Odyssey* becomes the first Penguin Classic published, and promptly sells three million copies. Suddenly, classic books are no longer for the privileged few.

1950s Rieu, now series editor, turns to professional writers for the best modern, readable translations, including Dorothy L. Sayers's *Inferno* and Robert Graves's *The Twelve Caesars*, which revives the salacious original.

1960s The Classics are given the distinctive black jackets that have remained a constant throughout the series's various looks. Rieu retires in 1964, hailing the Penguin Classics list as 'the greatest educative force of the 20th century'.

1970s A new generation of translators arrives to swell the Penguin Classics ranks, and the list grows to encompass more philosophy, religion, science, history and politics.

1980s The Penguin American Library joins the Classics stable, with titles such as *The Last of the Mohicans* safeguarded. Penguin Classics now offers the most comprehensive library of world literature available.

1990s The launch of Penguin Audiobooks brings the classics to a listening audience for the first time, and in 1999 the launch of the Penguin Classics website takes them online to a larger global readership than ever before.

The 21st Century Penguin Classics are rejacketed for the first time in nearly twenty years. This world famous series now consists of more than 1300 titles, making the widest range of the best books ever written available to millions – and constantly redefining the meaning of what makes a 'classic'.

The Odyssey continues ...

The best books ever written

SINCE 1946

Find out more at www.penguinclassics.com